Monster
without Mercy

New York Times & *USA Today* Bestselling Author

CYNTHIA EDEN

DEDICATION

For all the readers who are a bit like Buffy...and
you like a little "monster in your man" when you
open a book.

PROLOGUE

"When in doubt, be bad. It's so much fun."

-Life (and Death) Lessons from Xavier Hollow

"You have to be good," Micah Gray delivered the dreaded words to his king and then held his breath because he knew what would happen next. *I hope I don't get blisters. I hope—*

Fire flew from Xavier Hollow's fingers and slammed into the floor at Micah's feet. "You *know* how I hate that word. It gives me hives."

The flames had missed Micah. This time. He let his breath out and ran a hand across his sweaty brow. "Yes, I do know. But I'm afraid it's necessary." And the grand king of destruction was right. The "g" word was known to make red streaks slide over the powerful king's body. When he actually committed a "good" act, he suffered excruciating pain. Not that Xavier committed any particularly good acts. Not in centuries...More like millennia?

Sacrifice and kindness were just literally not part of his genetic makeup.

Darkness, evil, and mayhem? They were the king's bread and butter. But desperate times could call for some, uh, *good* measures. "The curse is going to kick in." A warning that the king should not need. But someone had to possess the courage to remind his wretched evilness of the problem at hand.

"Fuck the curse." Xavier twirled a ball of fire over his fingers.

Please do not throw that fire at me. There was a reason no one else had been brave enough to enter the throne room. The king always tossed fire when he got news he didn't like. *He will not like this.* "I'm afraid the, uh..." Micah took a step back. "Curse is going to fuck *you*, my lord."

Xavier's dark eyes narrowed. The ball of fire got brighter. Hotter.

"That is..." Micah yanked at his collar. It was way, way too tight. "The curse will take away your power. You've known about this for a long time—"

"Curses bore me. I'm too strong for them. Witches can cast whatever spells they want. But *I* am the king of destruction. I burn cities to the ground. I incinerate my enemies. I lay waste to—"

"This particular curse was put on you by your father, not some weak witch. You know that." He'd had to interrupt because once Xavier got going about his evil deeds, the king did tend to roll on and on. And on. "He, um, wanted you to prove yourself, remember?"

The flames came at him. Micah screamed and jumped out of the way. But he didn't jump fast enough or far enough and the fire caught his shirt.

He slapped at the flames. *Blisters. I'll have them on my fingers—*

"I remember everything," Xavier growled.

The flames winked out. His shirt smoked. His fingers stung. Dammit. "You, ah, remember that you can break the curse, right? Break the curse. Prove yourself to your father."

"My *father* is long dead."

Yes. Maybe. Hard to say for sure. "The curse isn't."

More flames began to dance over Xavier's hand. The flames were reflected in his eyes, turning the darkness to a deep red.

Oh, no. Micah spoke, again, fast. He burst out, "You just have to find someone *good.*" There. Done. Said.

Mocking laughter spilled from Xavier. "Have you taken a look at the human world lately?"

"You have three days, my lord. *Three.* When the clock strikes midnight tonight, the countdown officially begins." If time hadn't been running out, he never would have dared to face the king this way. But, there was a bright spot... "You have to find a woman with a soul of goodness and get her to sacrifice herself for you. She has to give you her soul, her life...or else you'll be power—"

"Do *not* fucking finish that sentence." Xavier leapt to his feet. The throne room trembled with his fury.

Powerless. Micah licked his lips. "I have good news." His voice cracked.

Another growl from Xavier. Micah winced. Sure, he was using the "good" word a lot, but it was necessary. Hurriedly, he added, "I've located the descendant of an angel."

In a blink, Xavier was in front of him. He grabbed Micah by his shirtfront and hauled him into the air. Since the king of destruction stood at around six-foot-four—when he was in human form, anyway—Xavier usually towered over Micah. Thus, the hauling him up to eye-level business.

"There are no angels on earth," Xavier told him flatly.

"Yes, you are correct. As you so often are." Xavier loved praise. "Wise. Ever so wise."

A grunt.

"But this is the *descendant* of an angel. And that's close enough, don't you think?" He sure hoped it would be. "Didn't even know she was out there, but one of your, ah, crew saw her on the street. He could see the shine in her."

Xavier's eyes widened.

The shine. Angels were so bright that you couldn't stare directly at them for very long. But the *descendants* of angels? The rare humans who'd been created by forbidden trysts with the creatures from heaven?

The descendants carried a faint shine. A glow that seemed to shine from within them. Only other paranormals could see that tell-tale glow.

"Where." Not a question, but a demand from Xavier.

"New Orleans." Plenty of sin lived in that city, so Xavier's minions had been well entrenched in the area. When one had spotted the descendant...

Xavier smiled.

Oh, no. I can see his fangs. Usually when you saw Xavier's fangs, it was a very, very bad sign. Micah braced for pain.

But Xavier just put Micah onto his feet.

The scary smile remained on the king of destruction's face.

I pity the descendant.

"Name," Xavier snapped.

"Her name is M-Mercy—"

More laughter spilled from Xavier.

"Mercy Josephine," Micah finished with a gulp. "And, she's going to be at a charity ball tonight—"

The laughter became louder. Then... *"Of course, she is."*

"It's...ah, a costume ball...you can...sneak in...get close to her...charm her..." Because the king could be charming, when he wanted to be.

All part of his power. Xavier Hollow could seduce anyone with barely an effort. Humans— and paranormals—fell at his feet. He was a master charmer and an epic destroyer. He could kill you even as you begged him to love you.

Evil.

Through and through.

Xavier opened his hand. The flames danced. "I'll have her in my palm. She'll gladly die for me." His hand closed, and he extinguished the fire. Smoke drifted from his fingers.

Micah swallowed. "Y-you'll have to act good..."

A muscle jerked along Xavier's square jaw.

"To fool her. To convince her to fall for you. You'll need to pretend to be like her." Because angels—or humans with a bit of angel blood—were always drawn to goodness.

And repelled by evil.

So Xavier's normal tricks wouldn't work. Mercy Josephine would feel uncomfortable around him, wary, so he'd have to work at convincing her that she could trust him.

That she could love him.

That she should give up her soul for him.

Three days. He *hated* to say it, but Micah whispered, "My king, time is ticking."

The king snapped his fingers. *Poof.* The king of destruction vanished.

Micah glanced around the throne room. *Gone.* Xavier could transport through dimensions in little more than a blink. Micah knew the king would be on his way to New Orleans. Off on the biggest hunt of his life.

"Good luck," Micah whispered.

Then he winced. There wasn't gonna be anything at all *good* about this endeavor.

For a moment, he almost felt sorry for Mercy Josephine.

CHAPTER ONE

"'No good deed goes unpunished.'
Don't know who originally said that shit, but I
want to punch him in the face."

-Life (and Death) Lessons from Xavier Hollow

An angel stood at the top of the staircase.

Xavier stiffened when he saw her. A picture of grace, beauty, and elegance...with giant, white wings springing from her back. Feathered wings. The wings matched the long, body-hugging, white dress that the angel wore. Sinful when she should have been going for virtuous. The angel must have missed a memo somewhere.

She stood up there, and her gaze swept the ballroom below her. She bit her lower lip. Ran a shaking hand over her perfectly straight, brown hair. Hair that fell just long enough to skim her delicate shoulders.

He couldn't see the color of her eyes. Mostly because she hadn't looked his way. She was too busy being all nervous and scared at the top of the stairs.

Then she started to descend. Little feathers trailed in her wake as they worked free of the wings and drifted in the air. She lifted one hand to tug up the too long hem of her dress, revealing shoes that were, again, sinful not virtuous. Three-inch heels. Spikes. Sexy.

He was already smiling even when the angel began to fall. One of those spiky heels caught on the back of her dress. Her mouth dropped open in surprise. And he knew she was about to take a serious header down those stairs. Down, down, she would go.

A broken angel.

She didn't even have time to scream.

One moment she began the tumble.

And in the next...

Xavier snapped his fingers.

He appeared right in front of her. He caught the angel, sparing her from savage embarrassment and brutally broken bones even as pain knifed through his gut.

No good deed ever goes unpunished. Fucking words that he had to live by.

Xavier hissed out a breath.

And her eyes locked on him.

Amber. Something he hadn't expected. A battered gold. Oddly enthralling.

She grabbed him. Her fingers curled along his arms as she held him tightly. "Thank you!" A gasp of relieved breath burst from her. "You saved my life!"

He shrugged. "Doubtful. Just might have spared you from a broken leg or arm." His nostrils flared. What *was* that scent? It came from her.

Sweet and heady at the same time. He brought his head closer to hers. Sniffed her. *Delicious.*

"Well, I am grateful." A shaking laugh spilled from her. "I didn't even see you there."

There. On the stairs? She hadn't seen him because he hadn't been there. He'd been all the way across the ballroom. Oh, but magic could be a glorious thing.

Her head tilted back as she beamed at him. "Please know that you are my hero."

He stiffened. "How dare you."

She blinked. "Excuse me?"

Shit. Fuck. He was supposed to be the hero. "How daring of you..." What was he supposed to say? "To wear such a...bold costume." The wings were massive. Truly. They took up most of the width of the stairs as they spread behind her.

She grimaced. "It's too much, isn't it?" She craned to look over her shoulder and sighed. "I did not ask for this. I wanted to be a witch. I *ordered* a witch costume. I was going to be dark and spooky." Her head turned back toward him. "Instead, when I unzipped the costume bag, this is what was waiting inside for me. Angel wings, a dress that is *way* too tight..."

He rather thought the dress fit perfectly, at least in certain places. Places like her high, full breasts, her flaring hips, her—

"And the shoes? I am going to break my neck in them." She hesitated. Then nodded. "Hold on." Her right hand left him, but her left clamped even more tightly around him. "No one but you has to know..."

Intrigued, he crooked a brow.

She took off her shoes. And sighed in relief. She also immediately dropped three inches and became even more fragile. At least, fragile to him.

"So much better." A bright smile lifted her full lips and made her amber eyes sparkle. "The dress is so long that no one has to know I'm not wearing shoes. It will just...well, I'll pretend the dress is supposed to be this way. Some sort of daring, dragging fashion." She let go of him. "And maybe I can get through this nightmare of a night after all."

Doubtful. "Nightmare?"

She looked out at the throng of people. The band had started to play again. "I don't like crowds," she confessed. "I tend to prefer quieter scenes."

He studied her profile as she stared at all the people. A good profile. Lovely. Not necessarily beautiful, but perfection had always bored him. A cute nose. Curving cheek. Her lips were truly intriguing. Full. A little naughty. And those eyes of hers...

She sent him a quick glance and blushed. "I am so sorry. I didn't mean to trap you with me." She angled her body to the side. The wings did not angle well. They went right on taking up all the space. "Thank you for saving me."

With her shoes in one hand and with the other hand holding up the hem of her dress, she headed down the stairs.

Darling, if you're lifting your skirt, everyone will see your bare feet. Didn't she get that? "Wait."

She looked back.

"Don't I get a name?"

Her laughter came again. As did her blush. Her laughter caught him off guard because it was strangely beautiful. Musical laughter.

"Mercy," she told him. "I'm Mercy Josephine."

"And I'm Xavier Hollow." He moved down a step so that he could be closer to her. His hand extended. "Pleasure to meet you."

Fuck. Even as the polite words rolled from his lips, he felt an itch on his back. *Hives.* His nostrils flared. He hated being good.

Her fingers curled with his, and warmth seemed to spread from her touch—spread from his hand all the way through his body. Xavier forgot about the hives. "It's not every day that I meet a real angel."

This time, she sent him a half-smile. "And it's not every day that I meet a vampire."

His tongue slid along one fang. He'd almost forgotten about the fangs.

"Those are quite impressive," she told him. "They look real."

Because they are. "Um. I can make them retract, too." And he did. The fangs could appear and disappear at will.

She gave a little gasp. "That's incredible."

Of all his talents, that one was the least incredible.

Her gaze darted over his attire.

"All black," she murmured. "How dark and foreboding. Totally what a vampire would wear."

Black to match his soul. *Oh, wait. I don't have one of those.* "Black is my favorite color."

Her smile came again. "Mine, too."

He stiffened.

"Nice mask, by the way."

The mask was a bit of carnival fun that had seemed to fit with the vibe of New Orleans. It covered the upper portion of his face. Plenty of other guests at the ball wore similar masks. There were humans in all sorts of costumes in the ballroom. Lots of sexy female demons. A glamorous ghoul or two. He'd caught sight of a mummy shortly after arriving. Had thought about stomping on the loose material hanging from the back of the costume and tripping the guy but...

But then I saw the angel at the top of the stairs. And he'd been spellbound.

She tugged on her hand and Xavier realized he was still holding it. Was, in fact, lightly stroking the back of her hand with his fingers.

"I...am supposed to go downstairs," Mercy told him. "My stepfather is sponsoring the ball, and I have strict orders to mix and mingle."

"We are mingling. Fuck mixing with anyone else."

Her incredible eyes widened.

Oh, had that not been polite? Xavier huffed out a breath. "Perhaps you will agree to dance with me. I did save you from a vicious fall, after all." In case she needed the reminder.

"I would love to dance with you."

The eagerness in her voice caught him by surprise. He hadn't even been using his charm power yet. *Oh, this is going to be so easy.* "Then let's go."

She started to practically bounce down the stairs. Since he couldn't have her dying—yet—he caught her arm and helped her in a more sedate fashion. Only when they were at the landing did he let her go. She took a few quick steps away and then turned back to him and—

Light.

A faint light seemed to fill the air around her. A glow. No, a *shine*. A sure sign of a descendant. The shine had, no doubt, been there all along. Only he'd gotten distracted by her wings. Her curves. Her smile. Her eyes.

What is my problem?

He'd missed the shine. There was no missing it now. Not when it seemed to push back against the darkness of the ballroom and fill all the space around her.

Mercy glanced around quickly, then she ditched her shoes behind a potted plant. Xavier felt something odd tugging at his lips.

A smile? A real one?

"I should warn you," Mercy said, voice serious but low, "I'm not a very good dancer."

"I don't care."

Her brows climbed. "Really?"

Absolutely. So low on his list of priorities. "Your dancing ability is the least important thing in the world to me right now." He began to pull her toward him and then—

"Mercy!"

Another man was in his way. A man with dark hair, intent, blue eyes, and wearing a black tux. No mask. Xavier could easily view his rather weak features.

"Mercy, we need you to go on stage," the man huffed. "You have to fill in and be the first auction participant."

Mercy's mouth dropped. "No, no, Thomas, I'm not supposed to be in the auction—"

What auction?

The guy sighed and put his hand on Mercy's shoulder.

Xavier stiffened. Someone should have told the man not to touch things that did not belong to him.

"Katie couldn't make it. There was an emergency at the hospital and she wasn't able to leave. Your stepdad needs someone to fill in for her." He sent her a jerky nod. "It's for charity. Look. Just go up there. Smile for the audience, and someone will bid on a date with you. The whole thing will be over in five minutes." Then he frowned at her. "Are you shorter? I swear, you were taller earlier—"

"She's missing shoes," Xavier told him helpfully. "And if you don't move the hand off her, you'll be missing it."

Now he had the jerk's attention. The man swung toward him. *"What?"*

Xavier smiled. "Your hand is still on her."

The guy lifted his hand, but only so he could point at Xavier. "Who are you?"

"Ah, isn't the point of a costume ball that my identity should be kept secret?" *Better question...who the fuck are you?* He believed that Mercy had called the man Thomas. They spoke with far too much familiarity.

Hmmm...*I may have to kill him.*

"I don't have time for this," the man hissed. "Mercy, get your shoes. Get on the stage. Your stepdad has done so much for you. Do this *one* thing for him, okay?" Then he stormed away, as if certain his orders would be followed.

Xavier's fingers twitched with the urge to throw a ball of fire after his arrogant ass.

"I'm sorry," Mercy said softly. "I need to go."

Of course, she didn't. "You don't need to do a damn thing."

A little exhale as her shoulders sagged. "You don't understand my life."

No, he didn't. And he wasn't there to understand her. He was there to get her to put her soul in the palm of his hand so he could crush it. But he should probably be acting like he *wanted* to understand her. So he attempted to seem patient and concerned.

"It can't be that bad," she muttered. "Five minutes and it will be done." She nibbled on her lower lip. "Save a dance for me, will you?"

Not like he was going to waste his time dancing with anyone else.

Mercy turned away.

His hand flew out and wrapped around her shoulder. In the exact place the jerk had been touching moments before. Her skin felt warm and soft. Delicate. "If you don't like crowds..." She'd told him that before. "Then I think you probably will hate being the center of attention for everyone here."

"Talk about a nightmare," she returned.

Oh, do tell me all about nightmares. He loved hearing those tales.

"But sometimes, we have to do things that we hate."

At those soft words from her, something twisted in his gut. He let go of her. He watched as she hurried toward the stage.

The man who'd ordered her up there—he was already reaching for a microphone. The band stopped playing as a spotlight fell onto him. Thomas.

Mercy stood on the edge of the stage, near other costumed people who Xavier supposed were also participating in this auction.

Mercy had no spotlight on her. Not yet. She didn't need one. Her shine lit her up.

So much goodness.

Odd, though. She'd shown no signs of being repelled by him. She should have. She should have been afraid to let him close. And when he touched her, she should have shivered in revulsion. She hadn't.

Why not?

What an interesting puzzle his Mercy was turning out to be.

"Ladies and gentlemen, thank you so much for coming out to the costume ball tonight!"

Oh, fabulous. The dick was talking.

"On behalf of Theodore Carlisle, I want to welcome you all to our celebration." The spotlight briefly flickered off the speaker and drifted into the crowd. It paused on an older man, no mask, with a broad grin. He wore a cape and had a sword strapped to his side.

The stepdad.

"I'm Thomas Durant, and I'll be the MC for the evening." The spotlight returned to the dick. Ah, to Thomas. "We've got some great volunteers up here who are auctioning off their time. Bid high enough, and you will be spending the evening with some of the best and brightest. A full dinner will be included with your bid. Lawyers, doctors, even a supermodel...you don't want to miss out, so get ready." He clapped his hands together. "Our first bid is actually Theodore's accomplished daughter Mercy." He gestured for her to come forward.

Slowly, she did.

She hadn't put her shoes back on.

Xavier smiled when she lifted up the hem of her dress a wee bit to walk, and he caught sight of her bare feet.

"Mercy is a Ph.D. candidate at Tulane. She knows more about ancient myths and legends than anyone I know." A rumbling burst of laughter poured from him. "Monsters fascinate her."

Xavier's lips parted in surprise. *Do they?* Well, he could certainly be fascinating...

And terrifying. Whatever the case needed to be.

"Bid on an outing with Mercy and you'll dine on a steamboat and enjoy a delicious New Orleans meal..."

Okay, enough of this. Mercy was shining extra brightly, and he could see her fingers trembling as she pushed back her hair. More feathers drifted around her as they fell from her fake wings. "Ten thousand dollars!" Xavier's voice thundered across the room.

"I—" Thomas stopped. He'd been rambling about something. "I-I hadn't started the bidding."

Who cared?

Xavier marched his way through the crowd. *Get the fuck out of my way.* They did. A little boost of magic helped to get them to back up. "I just finished it. Ten thousand dollars." He stopped at the bottom of the stage. "Now, sweetheart, how about that dance?"

Her amber eyes lit up. Her shine burned hotter. She hurried to the edge of the stage as if she'd just jump right down into his arms.

Fair enough. *So damn easy.* He opened his arms to her.

And that was when the screaming started.

Because he was staring at Mercy's face, he saw the shock that swept over her expression. Shock, horror. Terror.

The screams came from behind Xavier. So did the...*growls?* He whirled away from Mercy and the stage and gaped at the sight before him. Three *fully shifted werewolves* had burst into the ballroom. They were knocking into humans. Slashing with their claws as they raced for their target.

And their target...

Fuck. Are they coming straight at me?

Bad mistake. The worst mistake those mangy fools had ever made. He would—

One wolf jumped over him. Jumped up *toward* the stage. Toward Mercy. And understanding dawned too late.

The beasts are here for her.

Screw that shit. "I found her first," Xavier roared, and he caught the jumping wolf by the tail.

CHAPTER TWO

"Know what matters in this world? Strength. Power. Wipe the floor with your enemies. Just drag their entrails straight across the hardwood."

-Life (and Death) Lessons from Xavier Hollow

"Not real," Mercy whispered when she saw the giant wolves barreling across the ballroom. She'd taken her medicine that morning, hadn't she? She was sure the little pink pill had been beside her water at breakfast. Since her stepfather had found a doctor to prescribe those pills for her, she'd taken them religiously. Ever since her eighteenth birthday. She didn't miss a dose and she didn't see...

Monsters.

Only she was seeing them at that moment and people were screaming. And a big, giant *wolf* with a mouthful of dripping fangs was leaping toward her.

Not real. Not real. Not real.

She could feel his breath on her cheek. That sure *seemed* real.

Mercy closed her eyes.

She expected to feel the bite of those teeth as they ripped into her. But instead...

A whimper. A pain-filled howl. A—

She opened her eyes.

The wolf hadn't made it onto the stage with her. Instead, the beast was on the floor, with Xavier standing over him.

"You are *fucking* up my business!" Xavier snarled.

Two more wolves ran at him.

"Watch out!" Mercy cried.

Xavier whirled toward her. "You. Get the hell out of here. You're a big, freaking beacon for—"

The wolves slammed into him. Biting. Clawing.

She screamed.

They took Xavier down to the floor. The third wolf leapt back up and joined in the attack on him.

"No!" Mercy shouted. She started to leap off the stage—

"What in the hell?" A hard arm closed around her stomach and yanked her back. Feathers flew into the air. "Mercy, come on!"

Thomas. Thomas had jerked her back. He was hauling her away from the stage and the chaos. So much chaos. People were running for the exit and screaming, and Xavier was—

Burning?

Yes, yes, she could see smoke. "We have to help him!" She struggled against Thomas, but he just held her tighter. "Xavier!" Mercy yelled.

He threw the wolves off him. Rose to his feet. Thomas had her near the curtains at the back of the stage, and she grabbed one, trying to hold on so she could see Xavier.

His eyes locked on her.

Smoke drifted around him.

A wolf tried to bite him. Xavier drove his fist into the wolf's head.

Her mouth dropped open. That was—uh—

"Let her go!" Xavier's bellow.

But Thomas didn't let her go. He jerked harder. She lost her grip on the curtain and the last sight she had of Xavier—he was whirling to face another wolf.

"Wolves," she gasped. "You saw them, too? Everyone sees them?" *I'm not crazy?*

"Dogs," Thomas threw out. "A pack of wild dogs got inside the building. We're getting the hell out of here. Don't worry."

But she was extremely, terrifyingly worried. "My stepdad—"

"Already gone. He's safe. Don't worry," he told her again. His grip was like a band of steel around her stomach. He half-dragged, half-carried her toward the rear of the building.

She fought his grip every moment. "I am worried! Xavier needs our help!"

"Screw him," Thomas spat. "Messing up all our freaking plans."

What? What had he just—

Thomas yanked open the back door of the building. He practically tossed her through the doorway. She would have fallen onto her ass because of the too long dress but—

Xavier caught her. His hands locked around her shoulders. "You have trouble walking." He shook his head. "Or do you just fall a lot?"

"How—why—you—" He'd been behind her. Fighting the wolves—*dogs. Thomas said they are dogs.* She shook her head. "How are you here?" And then...*does it matter?* Mercy threw her arms around him and held on tightly. "I'm so glad you're okay!"

He tensed against her.

They were in an alley behind the building, an area that rather smelled of rot. She ignored the smell and the trash as relief coursed through her. *Xavier made it out.* "I wanted to help you!" Leaving him hadn't been her choice. "I was trying to help—"

"Yes, I saw when you attempted to fly down to me." He pushed her back. Raked her with a stare. Then whipped off her wings and tossed them to the ground. "Those don't work. Don't try flying again."

"I—"

He bent before her. And ripped off half of her dress. The bottom half. The silky material now ended at mid-thigh.

Her breath caught. "Uh, Xavier..."

"You keep tripping on the damn thing." He remained partially bent before her. "You have...nice legs."

She smiled down at his dark head. "I'm glad you're okay." But he wasn't. He was bleeding. Her hand touched his neck where she could see what looked like deep claw marks. Bite marks? "Xavier—"

"Ahhh!" A guttural cry of fury. One that came from behind her.

She spun around and saw Thomas charging at them. She'd forgotten about him. "Thomas, stop, this is—"

Thomas grabbed her and shoved her out of his way. Then he lifted his gun—*a gun!*—and aimed it toward Xavier. "You don't get her!"

She'd hit the ground after his shove, so she didn't exactly see what happened next, but suddenly Thomas hurtled through the air and slammed into the garbage cans a few feet away.

"I get whatever the hell I want." Xavier's cool reply.

Then he was in front of her. Extending his hand to her. "Did he hurt you?"

Mercy shook her head.

"Shall I hurt him?"

"I—no?"

His lips pursed. Thanks to the full moon overhead, she could see him—and his decisive nod—quite clearly. "I think I will," Xavier informed her. "It will be fun."

What?

A limo's engine growled as the vehicle pushed down the tight alley. The driver hopped out and opened the back door. "Got her?" he asked.

"Got her." Xavier hauled Mercy to her feet. "You're in danger. I can save you."

"I—"

"Mercy..." Thomas rasped. "Get *away* from him!"

She realized he still had his gun. He was bringing it up. Aiming it.

At me?

Xavier lunged into her path.

The gun exploded. The blast had her ears ringing and Xavier—he just started laughing.

"You've been shot!" Mercy cried out. Her terror-filled voice seemed to echo in the night. A person wasn't supposed to laugh when a bullet hit him. And *why* had Thomas fired that gun? "Xavier!" She grabbed his arm and yanked him toward her.

Blood covered his chest.

"No!" She put her hands over the wound. Tried to stop the blood flow, but it was impossible. He kept bleeding and bleeding and how was he remaining on his feet? He should be on the ground. They needed to get an ambulance.

"Let's go," Xavier told her. He didn't even sound winded. Didn't sound as if he—oh, had a *bullet in his chest.*

"But, but—" Mercy sputtered.

Sighing, he picked her up and carried her toward the open limo door.

"No issues?" the driver inquired pleasantly.

Xavier grunted.

Yes, yes, there were issues. Quite a few of them. And...

He'd gently put her on the seat inside the limo. "Stay there, will you?" Xavier dipped his head toward her. "Don't want to have to hunt you again."

"She does shine brightly," the driver muttered. "Think I need sunglasses."

What?

Xavier tucked a lock of hair behind her ear, then withdrew from the limo. She inched toward the open door.

"You sonofabitch..." Xavier's lethal voice. "Never come between me and what I want again. Understand me? *Never.*"

She tried to peer outside—

Whoosh.

Fire. She saw the flames—

Xavier slid into the vehicle. "Miss me?"

She couldn't speak. There was blood all over him.

The driver slammed the door. Through the window, she could see the flames dancing along the edge of the building. It looked as if they'd gone toward the line of garbage cans.

"He got away. Lucky bastard." Xavier edged closer to her. "Scoot to the side a bit, will you?"

She scooted. Her hands pressed over the seat and she realized... "I have your blood on me."

"Yes. I am bleeding quite a lot."

The limo was moving. She lunged for the little privacy screen that separated the back from the driver. Her shaking fingers found the button to lower it. As soon as the screen slid down, Mercy begged, "Get us to a hospital! Please! As fast as you can!"

The driver looked back at her. "Why?"

Why? *Why?* "Because he's dying!"

"Not today, he isn't," the man returned with basically zero concern.

"Micah," Xavier sighed, "just drive."

But—but—

Micah raised the privacy screen closed again. She stared blankly at it.

"I could use a little help," Xavier murmured.

She turned toward him. "What is happening?"

He sprawled against the seat. His arms were spread out beside him. A faint, soft glow of light poured from the floor of the limo to illuminate the scene. "I'm saving you," he told her. "Didn't you notice?"

"I—"

"Those werewolves were coming after you."

Her eyes closed. "Dogs."

"Uh, werewolves."

"Dogs."

"Dogs don't usually have teeth that long and possess supernatural strength. They also aren't usually the size of bears."

Wait, had they been the size of bears?

"I saved you," he said again. "Now you can save me."

Her eyes opened. "Am I hallucinating?" She must be. Maybe...maybe this whole night wasn't happening.

"I don't know." His head tilted to the side. Impossibly, he still wore the oddly seductive mask that somehow made his dark eyes seem absolutely magnetic. "Do you hallucinate a lot?"

Once upon a time, yes. "I see monsters."

Silence. "Is that what you're seeing right now? When you look at me?"

She didn't know what she was seeing. "You're wearing a mask, so it's hard to tell."

"Huh. Okay." His hands rose, and he tugged off the mask. A casual toss sent the mask sailing onto the seat next to him. "Better now?"

So. Much. Better. She'd seen his strong, square jaw before. But now she glimpsed the perfect blade of his nose. Could study his high, almost savagely sharp cheekbones. His face wasn't just handsome. It was...rugged. Sexy. Fierce.

His lips curled. "Like what you see?"

Yes.

"Not a monster, am I?"

"You don't look like one."

"And what do monsters look like?"

Her heart raced in her chest. It had been doing that ever since she'd heard the first scream back in the ballroom. "Sometimes, they have fire in their eyes. Fangs that explode in their mouths. Mostly, though, they have these thick, grim shadows that cling to them."

He surged forward and reached out for her. His hand clamped around her wrist. "You've seen monsters."

Was that a question? A statement? Either way, this wasn't the time to dive into a giant narrative about her hallucinations. *The man is bleeding out.* "You were shot." Where was the panic? The weakness? He seemed fine. "You need help."

His fingers stroked along her wrist. "I've already said you can help me." He tugged her closer.

She didn't even put up a fight. Part of her wanted to be close to him. Wasn't that weird? As weird and crazy as everything else had been that night.

He tucked her in against his side, and his left hand rose to push the hair away from her neck. His head lowered over her skin and he...inhaled. "What is that scent? Delicious."

Her heartbeat just pounded faster. "Are you talking about my body lotion? It's peaches and cream."

"Mind if I have a taste?"

A taste? Of her? Men didn't ask for tastes of her. Men didn't want tastes of her. No one approached her. They tended to avoid her like the plague. She stayed busy with her research and her files and she didn't try to date anyone. So why, *why* did she whisper... "Yes, please."

"So polite." His lips feathered over her throat.

This isn't happening. The werewolves weren't real. The sexiest man I've ever seen in my life isn't kissing my throat. And he doesn't have a bullet wound in his chest. None of this is real.

She was having another episode. One that was much, much worse than anything she'd experienced in years. "I'm losing my mind." Sadness. She'd always feared this. Ever since her mother's death. Tears pricked at her eyes. "Are you even real?"

"Oh, I'm very real. And it's not your mind that you'll be losing." His lips pressed to her throat again. "It's your heart."

Heat burned through her. A sensual energy that seemed to pulse through her veins. This wasn't happening, despite his words. This couldn't be real. This couldn't—

Pain. A pinprick at her throat. Then it was gone in a flash. Pain and pleasure blended for her in a mad, uncontrollable whirlwind. Pleasure knifed through her body, surged right to her sex, and a sudden, intense climax slammed through her body.

What is happening?

Her sex contracted, her body shook, and she choked out a scream.

Then oblivion took her. A complete, total, dark and sweet oblivion.

***

Mercy went limp in his arms. Her blood was on his tongue, her power filling him. Healing him. He'd *felt* her pleasure. No one had ever climaxed from his bite before.

His tongue licked over the small wounds he'd left on her throat, and his head lifted. He pulled her closer as he studied her.

"I'll be damned," he whispered. And smiled.

Yes, I will be. Have been...

And will be again.

The privacy screen rolled down. "Uh, my king?" Micah called.

Xavier pulled Mercy onto his lap and cradled her against him.

"Have you already accomplished your goal?" Micah wanted to know.

No, he hadn't accomplished the goal. He was fast, but not *that* fast. Xavier's gaze remained on her face. Such an interesting face. Those lips...he would like to taste them.

"You fed from her?"

He had. "Definitely a descendant." As if the shine hadn't been enough of a clue. He could *taste* her power, and, truth be told, it made him feel a little drunk.

He also sported one serious hard-on for her. Wincing, he shifted her a bit in his lap.

"Feeding isn't the goal," Micah pointed out.

Xavier rolled his eyes. "I know." He'd counted on Micah following him. The guy always did. So Xavier hadn't been surprised to see the limo roll down the alley. In fact, he'd thought...*perfect timing.*

"She needs to *sacrifice* herself for—"

They hit a pothole. The whole car jolted, and Mercy, with her eyes closed, gasped.

"Be more careful." He pulled her ever closer against him. "She could have fallen to the floor!"

Micah seemed to choke. Then, "Uh, my lord?"

"Be. More. Careful. Or I will rip off your freaking arms!" He gripped her tightly. "Take me to one of our houses here. Did you *see* those mangy werewolves? Hunting in public? Fully shifted?"

"That, ah, was unusual but—"

"They want her." Others had discovered what she was. "They won't get her. She's mine."

Silence.

The vehicle was now going very, very slowly. Probably because Micah didn't want his arms ripped off...again. It had taken them forever to grow back last time. Not that Xavier had been responsible for that particular injury. Sometimes,

Micah had a tendency to go after beasts that were stronger than he was.

But Xavier wasn't concerned about Micah and his silence. He was too fixated on Mercy. Why was she unconscious? Xavier frowned down at her. He hadn't taken a great deal of blood from her. Just sips really. His fingers fluttered over her neck to find her pulse.

"You...you meant she's your prey, right?" Micah finally stammered. "You meant to say...*she's my prey.*"

"Of course, I did." A relieved sigh slipped from him. Her pulse pounded in a steady rhythm beneath his touch. "What the hell else would I have meant?"

"What, indeed?"

"Drive the fucking car."

"Yes, my wicked evilness. Driving the fucking car."

"And make sure we're not being followed."

"You could just *snap* yourself away if you're worried about enemies following you."

He could snap. She couldn't. And he couldn't transport someone who was human—or *mostly* human—with him when he snapped. If he tried that, her body would basically explode.

He'd seen it happen.

He'd even deliberately used the technique on enemies.

"I'm not leaving Mercy." Flat. Final.

"I could bring her to you," Micah offered. "You do your poof thing, and we'll be there to meet you soon."

"I'm not leaving Mercy." Xavier knew he'd spoken clearly before, and Micah was well aware that he didn't like to repeat himself.

"Okay." Micah coughed. "Did you knock her out? She's kinda small. Was that really necessary?"

"I did not hurt her."

Micah slammed on the brakes.

Xavier held tightly to his prize and thought about incinerating his long-time guard and advisor. The scent of smoke filled the interior of the limo.

"If you didn't *hurt* her," Micah spun around to gape at him. "Then why is she unconscious?"

Pain wasn't the cause. "Pleasure," Xavier replied with a smug smile. He'd felt her tremble with her release. "My bite brought her so much pleasure she passed out."

Micah shook his head. "That shit doesn't happen."

"You're questioning *my* word?" He could burn Micah's shirt. Make sure the fire didn't spread to the rest of the car. Let the flames lance him. "It *did* happen."

"No, no, what I meant—you don't *give* pleasure to anyone. Your bite has never, in the history of *ever*, brought someone pleasure. That's not how it works with you."

Unease stirred within Xavier because Micah was right. Even as he'd dipped his teeth into Mercy's tempting neck, he'd known that he would hurt her. But...

But I hadn't wanted to hurt her.

He'd just been bleeding out. And if the blood loss had continued, he would have weakened. With enemies close by—enemies who seemed intent on taking her—he hadn't been able to afford any weakness.

Micah kept gaping at him.

"Drive the car," Xavier ordered.

"But—"

"Drive the car or lose the arms."

Micah drove the car.

And Xavier tried to figure out how he'd given Mercy pleasure, when he'd only been made to bring pain to someone like her.

CHAPTER THREE

"Burn your enemies to the ground. Then bring marshmallows for the fire. Everyone loves s'mores. Well, except for the enemies who are dead."

-Life (and Death) Lessons from Xavier Hollow

Her eyes flew open, and Mercy quickly realized two things.

One...she was not in her bed.

Two...she was not alone.

A man curled next to her. His hair was dark, mostly, but blond streaks rose from the depths of his thick mane. He was big. More like enormous, as he pretty much covered most of the bed. No shirt. Just a powerful, tanned chest. Black, silk sheets dipped below his waist. A faint line of stubble covered his hard jaw, and his long, thick eyelashes seemed to cast shadows across his cheeks.

Actually, for a moment, a big shadow seemed to stretch from his entire body, and that shadow reached out to her—

Mercy sucked in a sharp breath.

His eyes flew open.

Red. His eyes are red.

She blinked.

And his eyes were back to being dark. Such a deep, dark brown.

A warm smile spread over his lips. "Good morning, gorgeous."

Morning? It was morning? Where had the entire night *gone?*

He yawned. "You sure slept like the dead."

"Where am I?" She sat up and realized that she wore a T-shirt. Black. Soft. Big. *Oh, no.* Was the shirt his? "Where are my clothes?" Mercy's voice came out squeaking.

"Pretty sure the angel costume is a pile of ash somewhere."

"What?" She grabbed the covers and yanked them up. Her legs were bare. *Please, please let me have on underwear.* Her hand dipped beneath the covers and between her thighs.

"What *are* you doing?" He quirked a brow. His eyes gleamed wickedly. "And do you need any help?"

"I'm wearing panties." Her head sagged forward. "Thank goodness."

He growled. "You're wearing panties. What a bore. They should have been burned with the costume."

Her hand flew from beneath the covers. "You seriously burned my costume?"

A shrug. "You told me you never wanted to see it again."

"I—" She had no memory of that. "Did?"

He nodded. Then squinted at her. "You do remember who I am, don't you?"

Like she could ever forget him. "You're Xavier."

His slow smile came again. It made her toes curl. Xavier nodded, apparently pleased. "Glad to know you retained some highlights from last night."

She didn't know that she'd call them highlights. "How did I get in this T-shirt?"

"Well, when you stripped off the angel costume..."

"*I* stripped it off?" Mercy distinctly remembered him ditching her wings. And later...he'd torn half the bottom off the costume.

"I would have offered to help—gentleman that I am—but you unzipped the dress and dropped it before I could. Then, you know, fire came."

Breathe. Nice, deep breaths. Her shoulders squared. "I don't remember that part, either."

"You kept on your ever-so-virginal white bra and panties. No worries on that score. But since you told me black was your favorite color, I gave you a black T-shirt to wear."

"That was..." Mercy licked her lips. "Nice of you."

"Wasn't it?" He scratched at his shoulder. What looked like a red streak of hives had appeared on his tanned skin.

She swallowed. This was gonna be awkward but... "Was I drunk last night?"

His dark eyes just held hers.

"I don't usually get drunk, but I was nervous about having to attend the ball. That sort of thing really isn't my style." Understatement. That sort of thing had been more like one of her personal versions of hell.

He kept staring.

"So I had a glass of champagne. One glass. It shouldn't have made me..." Her voice trailed away. *Made me what? Strip? Pass out? Lose chunks of my night?*

Xavier wasn't helping her. His gaze just seemed to bore right into her very soul.

She should get out of the bed. Go home. "This has been...interesting." *Terrifying.* She hauled the sheet with her as she made a less than graceful exit from the king-size bed.

Only when she pulled the sheet, Xavier was left *uncovered*. And she saw that he only wore a pair of black boxers. *He really likes black.*

"I wore them for you." Again, he scratched at his shoulder. "Thought you'd freak if you woke up and I was naked, though, in my defense, you *did* tell me to get comfortable before you drifted off to dreamland."

Her mouth was open. She snapped it closed and yanked the sheet around her body. It moved with a soft slither. "I shouldn't be here."

"No, you shouldn't be standing there. You should still be in bed. We should be having slow, amazingly awesome, morning sex."

Heat flamed in her cheeks.

"Do you remember coming for me last night?"

Oh, no. That part wasn't a dream? The sturdy floor beneath her feet refused to open up and swallow her. Even when she pushed her feet down extra hard.

"All I did was put my mouth on your neck. A little bite." He sat up. His muscles flexed wonderfully. "And you were coming in my arms."

She had. The heat in her cheeks intensified. "I don't do that."

"Come for strangers?" A nod. "Thanks for telling me. But I'm not a stranger. I saved your life. At least twice. Maybe three times. You may appreciate me and my bravery forever."

Mercy backed away. Her gaze swung frantically around the room. Antique furniture. Gray walls. Black curtains drawn over the windows. No photographs. Zero personal touches. "I don't...don't *come* and then pass out."

"Ah, so you admit that you *did* come for me. And don't you want to do it again?" He winked.

Arousal surged through her. An arousal she should one hundred percent not be feeling, no matter how perfectly sexy he was. "You are dangerous."

His features hardened. The faint teasing that had lit his dark eyes moments before vanished. "Never forget that."

More memories flooded through her mind. Memories that couldn't possibly be real. *Werewolves?* No. Not. Real. "I need to get home." Immediately. Fear pulsed through her. "What time is it?"

"Early," he assured her.

Oh, thank goodness. Her shoulders fell. The dark curtains blocked out all the light. But if it was still early, then she hadn't missed her medicine and everything would be—

"Barely eleven a.m."

"Eleven a.m.?" She ran for the curtains and yanked them open. Bright light immediately poured into the bedroom.

"No!" A sharp cry from Xavier. "The daystar! I'm burning, *burning!*"

She whirled toward him.

He laughed. "Got you."

"What is happening here?"

"I don't know." His head cocked. "I think I just told a joke. Was it not funny?"

Her head shook. "I have to get home. Now." She rushed for the bedroom door. Hauled it open. Then she pretty much ran blindly because she had zero idea of where she was going. Mercy had a quick visual of a giant home. A big chandelier. Her gaze locked on a spiral staircase, and she hurried to it. Her bare feet thudded down the steps, but she dropped the sheet because the last thing she wanted was to trip.

She did that too much as it was.

Wearing just the T-shirt and her underwear, she reached the bottom of the stairs, then turned to the left. Then spun toward the right. Which way led to the front door?

Mercy took a few quick steps to the right.

And she slammed into Xavier. A fully dressed Xavier, wearing—shocker—a black shirt and pants as he blocked her path. "Boo," he whispered.

She bit back a scream. Then... "Stop it!" Mercy fired off a glare at him. "Stop scaring me, and how did you—" Her eyes widened. *How had he gotten down here so quickly? And gotten dressed so quickly, too?* She looked back toward the stairs.

He had not been behind her. She would have heard him on the steps. Wary, her stare flickered to him. "What is happening here?" Mercy was sure she'd asked that same question before.

But she knew. She knew with sudden, horrifying certainty exactly what was happening.

She'd missed her medicine. That day, and...had she missed it the day before, too?

Are the hallucinations back?

"Why are you running from me?" Xavier asked.

"Because I need to get home."

"Why?"

"Because...home is safe." *Home is where my medicine is.*

"Safe is boring." His hand lifted, and his knuckles slid down her cheek in a gentle caress. "Aren't you tired of a boring life? I could give you so much more." He leaned toward her. "I could show you things most people only fantasize about. Give you more pleasure than you can stand. I can rip away the veil, and you'll see wonders that you will never forget."

Her breath shuddered out. "Your touch does strange things to me."

His long, thick lashes flickered. "Does my touch make you want to run from me?"

"No." Maybe that was one of the things that scared her. "It makes me want to get as close to you as I can."

His eyes—so dark and deep—widened in surprise.

"But I don't know you. I don't spend the night with men I don't know, even if those men give me a great orgasm and save my life." She spun away from him. *Where is the door?*

"You *did* spend the night with me. Rather too late to put that genie back in its bottle."

Her shoulders stiffened. "Were there...giant dogs at the ball last night?" *Dogs, not werewolves.* Her right hand rubbed her throbbing temple. "Did they attack everyone?"

"No, there were no dogs at the ball." Utter certainty filled his words.

Her shoulders slumped. Right. Of course, a pack of giant dogs hadn't erupted inside the fancy ballroom. She'd imagined them. The strongest hallucination she'd had in years. Tears filled her eyes, but she blinked them away. Maybe it wasn't about missing a dosage. Maybe the medicine just wasn't working any longer. "You should stay away from me. For your own protection." *Because what if I become dangerous now?* She took a surging step forward.

"They weren't dogs. They were werewolves."

Every muscle in her body froze.

"They don't usually show themselves to humans that way. Damn odd. But then, they were in a frenzy. Desperate for their prey. I suppose they thought desperate times justified desperate measures. Werewolves tend to be creatures driven more by emotions and primal needs. Not exactly the best critical thinkers out there."

She whirled toward him. "You're...joking again?"

"No, I only had one joke in me." Deadpan. His eyes gleamed. "Werewolves came for you."

Her bare feet inched back toward him. "Werewolves aren't real," she whispered to him.

He lifted his hand and crooked his finger at her, a silent sign urging her closer.

She crept closer.

"Of course," he whispered right back to her, "they are. If they weren't real, then I wouldn't have needed to kick their asses last night, now, would I?"

Mercy stared at him. At that devilishly handsome and darkly dangerous face. Then she lifted her right hand and used her fingers to pinch the skin of her left forearm.

A furrow appeared between his brows. "What are you doing?"

"Trying to wake up."

"Sweetheart, you are awake. Life is a nightmare."

A shiver skirted down her spine. "Werewolves aren't real."

He leaned so close she thought he intended to kiss her. "Do you think if you say that enough, it will be true?"

She wanted his mouth. "Y-you kissed my neck last night." He'd kissed her neck, and she'd come. She'd—

He shook his head. *No.*

Mercy blinked.

"I didn't kiss you. I bit you." Once more, his hand rose, and his knuckles lightly stroked down her cheek. "Maybe I did a bit of both."

Her heart slammed hard into her chest.

"I needed blood, you see, because that jackass with you shot me. Your blood helped me heal faster."

Her mouth dropped open. Her heart kept slamming hard into her chest.

He gave her a gentle smile. "Are you all right?"

She shook her head. *No.*

He kept stroking her cheek. "It's because of the blood part, yes? Probably shouldn't have told you that I drank your blood."

"You definitely should not have." Hushed.

"Because it terrified you."

Mercy managed to nod. "Because I am about to run screaming from this house."

His mouth kicked up into a half-smile. "You're not running yet."

"I think you're a hallucination." Sad. So sad. Her lips curled down. "I think I've gone crazy."

His half-smile faded. "Why would you ever think that?"

"Because it happened before." If he wasn't real, she could tell him everything. And he couldn't be real. A real man wouldn't have healed so quickly from a gunshot wound. In the bedroom, when she'd glimpsed his powerful chest, there had been no sign of any injury. Just rippling muscles. And a real man wouldn't drink her blood.

That was what vampires did.

Monsters.

"I'm an expert on monsters," Mercy confessed.

"Um, do tell." His hand dipped down and slid under her chin. He tipped her head back.

"They're what I study. Myths and monsters. I've learned everything that I can about them." They were her obsession. Had been, since her mother had died.

"You've learned everything that you could, but all that knowledge just came from books."

"I've studied other cultures. Legends. Art. I've researched and pulled everything together that I can. For centuries, humans have feared the things in the dark." Once again, she licked her lips. Fear kept making them go dry.

His gaze fell to her mouth. Lingered.

"I started fearing things in the dark when I was eighteen years old. That's when a pack of monsters killed my mother in front of me."

His stare flew back to capture hers.

"But monsters aren't real." What the cops and the doctors and her stepfather had told her over and over again. "I had a psychotic break. I saw them when they weren't there. My mom was killed in a robbery. Men killed her, not monsters. I have to take my medicine so I don't see the monsters again."

A muscle jerked along his suddenly clenched jaw. "Who put you on this medicine?"

"My stepfather."

"I'll kill him for you." A seemingly casual offer.

Her breath choked out. "I don't want you to do that."

He shrugged. *Shrugged*. His thumb began to lightly stroke over her lower lip. "You may change your mind. Just know, the offer will stand."

If he had been real, his words would have terrified her. But since he wasn't real... "You're the best hallucination I've ever had."

"I'll be the best everything you've ever had." Absolute arrogance. "But tell me more about the monsters you see."

"They can look like everyone else, but they have these thick, heavy shadows that cling to them. The shadows will twist and take on shapes. They can be horrifying." Snakes. Creatures with mouths bursting with razor-sharp teeth. "The shadows always reach for me." Her tongue slipped out. Accidentally touched his thumb.

"Of course, they do. You shine too bright."

She had no idea what that meant, but, before she gave in to her madness, Mercy did have one request. "Will you kiss me?"

"Why?"

"Because you're my favorite hallucination. All the others that will come after you will only get worse. I'd like to remember a good one."

"Fucking *hate* that word," he growled.

Which word? Oh, must be "hallucination." She probably shouldn't call him that. She should probably not ask him to kiss her, either. He wasn't real, and she was just giving into full-blown madness at this point. She was—

"Mercy?"

"Yes?"

"I'm very real."

Her lashes fluttered.

"And I will be the only one to kiss you from here on out." With that, his mouth took hers. His thumb had slid away, only to be replaced by the warm, passionate touch of his lips. He kissed her slowly, deeply, sliding his tongue into her mouth as he seemed to carefully taste her.

There was no rush. No frenzy. He took his time, as if she was some treat that he intended to savor. She'd been kissed before. Awkwardly as a teen. Hurriedly as an adult. Even enjoyed a few of what she'd thought were *good* kisses.

But this...

Wasn't good.

Her hands rose to curl around his shoulders even as she pressed onto her toes in order to get closer to him.

Xavier's kiss was a hundred times better than *good*. A thousand times. He pulled a response from her. A hot, aching response that had her nipples tightening, her sex aching, and her whole body shuddering as if she'd just suddenly jolted to life. For the first time, she seemed to *feel* everything. Every cell, every muscle, every nerve. Everything came alive with a burst of longing and need that ripped right through her.

The whole world seemed to shudder beneath Mercy's feet.

Just from a kiss.

And that sealed the deal for her.

The hands that had grabbed him slowly pushed him back. Her tongue teased his just once more, then she was pulling her head away and lowering her feet flat on the floor.

Xavier's expression seemed a bit dazed as he stared down at her.

"That proves you aren't real," she told him, truly sad. "Because no kiss has ever made me feel that way." Mercy squared her shoulders. "I was always warned this would happen sooner or later. I wished for later. But at least I had you to lead me into the dark." Then, giving into a strange impulse, she rose onto her toes once more. Only this time, her lips pressed to his cheek. "In my madness, I will miss you."

Even though they'd just met.

She pulled away even as she felt his fingers rising to curve around her waist. Mercy spun away from him and ran to the left. A door waited there. She yanked it open—

A wind seemed to rush over her body.

Mercy looked down and saw clothes covering her. Jeans. Tennis shoes. The same black T-shirt she'd worn before.

She laughed because clothes didn't magically appear on you.

Not unless you were losing your mind again.

She walked into the sunlight and didn't look back. What was the point? If she'd looked back, Xavier wouldn't have been there.

He couldn't be.

He was never real.

***

"My most fearsome king?" Micah cleared his throat because Xavier was just standing in the open doorway and *watching* the cure to his curse walk away. "Do you not feel the urge to...I don't know...give pursuit?"

He'd caught the end of the kiss. Had been pleased with the king's progress. Pleased, but not surprised. Xavier could charm the pants off anyone.

But... "She's getting away."

And Xavier kept watching her leave.

Micah crept closer. Perhaps he was missing something. "Oh, you put jeans on her. That was kind..."

A growl.

"Kind of an unnecessary move," he rushed to say.

Xavier turned his head toward Micah. Glared.

"Kind of...sneaky?" Micah coughed and tried to correct himself. "Kind of a diabolical move to get her to believe you are all things *good—*"

Another growl.

Sonofabitch. He could not win. "Fine! *Why* did you put full clothing on her? Why not just let her walk away half-naked?"

"Because others don't get to see her that way."

Uh, oh. Micah's eyes narrowed. "That almost sounded possessive." The king had always been bad about *not* sharing his toys.

"They're drugging her."

"Who is they?" Micah was missing a whole lot.

"Her stepfather. Probably the asshole who works for him—the one who shot me. Thomas something." He looked back through the open door again. "She's going right back to them now."

All the more reason to give pursuit. "Why are you letting this happen?"

"She thinks I'm not real."

Micah snorted out a laugh. "She'll wish you weren't real..." His words trailed away. Xavier's face had just gone extra hard. Hell. "You're about to throw flames at me, aren't you?" He backed up a quick step. This was his favorite shirt!

"What pill will stop her from seeing monsters?"

Micah tugged at his collar. "I am not following this conversation, your evilness."

Xavier's jaw clenched even more. "When Mercy was eighteen, she saw monsters murder her mother."

"Oh, yeah. That would make sense." He nodded. Total sense. "It was listed a knife attack during a robbery in the reports I read, but monsters probably ripped her mother apart if she was shining, too."

Xavier's eyes went straight *red*. "No one will be ripping apart Mercy."

Micah gestured toward the door. "You should probably go after her then. That is, if you don't want someone else ripping her apart." *Can we get some movement, here?* "She's weak. You're all powerful. A raging inferno of destruction. If you want the others to stay away, you just have to remain close to her. She'll think you're a hero. You'll be the threat she never sees coming. Genius. Utter evil genius." Was that enough flattery? Would Xavier get moving? *We need to hurry this along.* Time kept right on ticking.

"I won't let them drug her any longer. She will have the truth." Xavier lifted his hand.

"Um, when you say the truth—" Micah began.

Xavier snapped his fingers and vanished.

"Sonofabitch," Micah muttered. "Haven't you heard that humans don't deal so well with the truth?"

Especially when the truth in question wrecked their worlds.

CHAPTER FOUR

*"How do I deal with my enemies? I certainly
don't kill them with kindness. I burn them to the
ground instead. Much more efficient. Next
question."*

-Life (and Death) Lessons from Xavier Hollow

"Mercy!"

As soon as she opened the door to the house
on Richmond Place, Mercy found Thomas waiting
for her. He lunged off the couch and grabbed her
arms. His fingers bit into her skin as he told her,
"I was so worried when you didn't come home last
night!"

Home. Yes, this place was her temporary
home. A rental she'd gotten because she hadn't
wanted to stay with her stepfather. The location
on Richmond Place was convenient for her
studies at Tulane, and the neighborhood had
seemed quiet and safe.

Moments before, she'd taken the key from the
fake rock on her porch and let herself inside.
Mercy had no idea where her purse or phone had
gone. Had she taken them with her in the limo

when she fled with Xavier the previous night? She didn't think so. Maybe her belongings were still in the historic building, at the check-in desk she'd visited after arriving at the ball?

She'd used the trolley to get home, taking some money from a kind older lady who'd taken pity on her in order to pay the fare.

"Where were you?" Thomas's fingers bit deeper into her skin. "Your father and I have been worried sick! Carlisle gave me his key and asked for me to come here today, hoping you would show up." A brief pause. "Where were you?" he snapped again.

"I—" *Spent the night with a stranger.* No. She cleared her throat. Better not give him that response. "Was there an animal attack at the ball last night?"

"You're having hallucinations again." Flat. He did not let her go.

"Did…" *Ask the question. Just get it out.* "Did you shoot someone last night?"

"Of course, I didn't." His stare never wavered. "Mercy, have you been taking your pills?"

"I-I don't remember if I had one yesterday. And I definitely haven't had one today and—" A sharp cry of pain burst from her because his hold dug in so deeply.

"Enough of that," Xavier announced.

Xavier.

Because he was just suddenly lounging in the middle of her den. Arms thrown back over the edges of her sofa, his feet propped up on her coffee table.

She blinked, but he remained. A very vivid hallucination. "Not real," she whispered.

"Oh, I'm one hundred percent real, sweetheart. We talked about this."

And, sure enough, Thomas let her go and whirled toward Xavier. *Thomas sees him, too.*

"Get the fuck out!" Thomas bellowed.

"If I don't, will you shoot me again?" Casual. Mildly curious.

And Thomas—he was already pulling out a gun. He'd been wearing a gray suit, and the gun had been hidden beneath the elegantly cut jacket. Since when had he started carrying a gun? And *why* was he pointing it at Xavier? "No!" Mercy yelled. Then she slammed her body into Thomas's because she was not going to let him shoot Xavier again.

She and Thomas crashed to the floor. The gun exploded and, at first, she couldn't hear anything after that echoing blast of thunder. Her ears hurt and silence seemed to smother her and then—

A roar.

A bellowing roar of rage and retribution as Thomas was hauled off her and tossed across the room. He slammed into her bookshelf, and the books went flying.

Xavier crouched in front of her. "The bullet did *not* hit you."

It wasn't a question, but she still shook her head. "No."

"Of course not, it wouldn't have dared." His knuckles skimmed over her cheek. "Stay here while I kill him for you." He surged up and whirled away.

Stay here while I— "No!" She jumped to her feet, too. Xavier was rushing straight for Thomas, so she grabbed Xavier from behind and locked her arms around his waist. "Xavier, no! I don't want you killing anyone!"

"But, darling, the man deserves a good killing. Let me just rip his head off. Or put his insides on the outside. That will be fun. Or I could burn his flesh from his bones..."

"Oh, Christ!" Thomas tried to make a run for it. He surged away from the bookshelf and raced toward the door.

But suddenly there was a ball of flames—a ball about the size of a basketball—in his path. Hovering directly in front of his face.

"Move an inch," Xavier warned him, "and your flesh will start burning away."

Thomas did not move.

"Let go, sweetheart," Xavier urged her. "As much as I do enjoy it when you touch me, I have work to do." His fingers slid over her hands and unhooked her arms from his waist. He turned toward her.

Her breath choked out as shock rolled through her. "Your eyes are red."

"The better to unleash hell on earth."

How was she supposed to respond to that? *"Xavier?"*

"Take the pill!" Thomas yelled. But he hadn't moved his body forward. The ball of fire kept dancing before him. "Take the pill and you won't see monsters any longer!"

"Oh, she'll always see me." Xavier took his time strolling across the room. He moved behind the ball of flames and lifted his hand. The ball twirled over his open palm. "The pill trick might have worked for a time, but you can't hide the truth forever. We know what she is. The others are coming for her. Stupid mistake, bringing her to New Orleans. Unless...unless you *wanted* to put her out as prey?" The flames flared higher. "That why you pranced her up on that stage last night? Was the auction bit for real? You think you're gonna sell her to the highest bidder?"

Despite the *flames* right there in her den, goosebumps rose on Mercy's arms. "Xavier? What's happening?"

"Take your pill," Thomas gritted out. "It's an extra strong one. You are in the middle of a waking nightmare. You take the pill and things will get better. I put the pill on the coffee table for you. Just take it."

She could see the pill. And even a small glass of water. She just hadn't noticed the pill and water when she'd first burst into the home because Thomas had blocked the sight when he'd grabbed her.

"Take it!" Thomas yelled at her.

"Fuck yourself," Xavier returned. "Mercy, I'm real. These...these are real."

Her gaze jerked to him.

Just in time to see his fangs descend. Razor sharp.

"I bit you with them last night," he told her. He stared straight at her. The ball continued to spin in front of Thomas's face.

Her hand rose to touch her neck. The skin felt tender.

"The werewolves were real," Xavier added. "They'll be coming for you as soon as it's dark again. All the monsters will. You'll shine even brighter in the dark. I think this fucker..." The flames edged closer to Thomas. "He wants them to come for you. You're trying to sell her, aren't you? Foolish mistake. I made the bid last night. I won her. Hear me well. She. Is. Mine. And I will rip apart anything or anyone who tries to take her from me."

Her steps were slow as she skirted the coffee table and headed to Xavier's side. His eyes were so red. Redder than the flames. "What are you?" she breathed.

"I'm destruction." He sent her a smile, one that showed his fangs. "Sweetheart, what do you want me to destroy for you first? Him? The bastard who has kept you believing that you're crazy all these years? Your stepfather? He did the same thing. I can take them out with a thought."

Thomas...whimpered.

"I'll destroy the wolves," Xavier offered. A casual offer. Like he was just telling her he could take out the trash. "Annihilate their whole pack. No one fucks with what belongs to me."

Her temples ached. The throbbing got worse with every word. "I don't want you destroying anything for me."

"Fine. I'll do it for shits and giggles."

She reached out and touched his arm. He was solid and warm beneath her fingers. "You are real."

"Your own walking, talking nightmare." The red flared hotter in his gaze. "You aren't crazy.

You're just prey. Monsters are drawn to you. Probably were drawn to your mother, too. You really saw them kill her. You didn't imagine a damn thing."

You aren't crazy. How long had she desperately wanted someone to tell her those words?

"I'm betting the pill did more than make you stop seeing the shadows and beasts, didn't it?" Xavier asked with a knowing smile. "It stopped your light from shining so brightly."

"I don't know what you mean."

"Clearly." He looked back at Thomas. "But you do, don't you?"

"I'm protecting her."

"She has a new protector. Consider yourself fired." Then he laughed. "Another joke, Mercy. Did you hear that? Fired...because I'm gonna set this asshole on *fire.*"

She shook her head. "No." Soft.

"Mercy, take the pill! It protects you!" Thomas lifted his chin. "Take it...*then run!*"

Her hand didn't leave Xavier. "You have a terrible sense of humor," she told him. "We have to work on that."

"I've never tried to be funny before." He frowned and glanced her way. "You...do not like it?"

"I don't like the flames. Make them go away." Then. *"Please."*

His jaw locked, but he closed his hand into a fist. The flames vanished. Smoke drifted from his fingers.

"Run, Mercy," Thomas urged her. "He'll kill me, but you'll be safe. And if you can take your pills...*they won't see you.*"

"Naughty Mercy." Xavier reached out and tucked a lock of her hair behind her left ear. "You've missed a few pills, haven't you? That's why we can all see you."

"I don't know what that means." *See you.*

His hand slid down, moving slowly until it rested over her chest. "You carry a shine. I can see it coming from you. Like a big light that illuminates you. Bad things want to destroy light. It's the way of the world."

Her breath stuttered out. "But you can protect me?"

"I can keep the other monsters away from you. I'm stronger than they are. And I don't share." His hand slipped away. "Thomas, you bore me. Go to sleep and don't wake up until we're gone."

Just like that, Thomas flew across the room, landed on the couch, and appeared to immediately fall asleep.

"How—" Mercy began.

"Magic."

She squared her shoulders. "I'd like more of an explanation than that."

"Fine. I can bend space and time. I can also exercise an easy compulsion on those who are psychically weak. Your *friend* is weak. Happy now?"

"Happy is not the word I'd use." A million knots seemed to be in her stomach. "Terrified is better." She backed up a step. Then another. "You still have your fangs out. Are you...are you going to bite me again?"

"Probably. You taste delicious."

Another step back.

He let out a long-suffering sigh. "Oh, come on. It was good for you, too."

One more step back.

His gaze fell to the floor. "I don't...like it when you retreat from me." He seemed confused. "Are you afraid of me?"

"You just had fire spinning from your fingertips. You have fangs. You drank my blood." She cast a quick glance at the couch. "And you put Thomas under a spell."

"Compulsion."

"Semantics," she tossed back. Her hands clenched into fists then released, only to clench again—over and over—at her sides. "I'm dealing with a lot at the moment. I thought I was having hallucinations, but it turns out that monsters are...real?"

"Super real. You slept with one last night."

I came for one last night.

He rolled back his shoulders. "I'm sure the others know where you live. We should expect an attack at any moment. While the werewolves—and any vamps in town—will wait for nightfall, there are plenty of other beasts who can come for you during the day. I can't snap with you—"

"What's a snap?"

"It's when I jump from one location to another. Like, I'm here now. I snap, and I'll be in Mexico. Micah—you met him last night, he was driving the limo—he calls it snapping because I usually snap my fingers before I vanish." A roll of one shoulder. "He got me to start snapping ages ago. Said he needed a warning before I disappeared on him."

Was the room spinning? Or was she? "Right." Dazed. "A snap." She snapped her fingers.

"You can't snap," he told her. "You're human. Mostly. I can't snap you with me. So if the monsters come, I'll have to fight them."

"Why do monsters want me?"

He looked upward. "I told you already, you have a shine—"

"*Why?*"

"Because you have an ancestor who was an angel."

She fell on her ass.

Before she could even blink, he was in front of her. He'd disappeared and then reappeared and was reaching down to take her hand.

Mercy opened her mouth—and screamed.

CHAPTER FIVE

*"The best kind of enemy is a dead enemy.
Even if they resurrect later, zombies are idiots
who can't fight for shit."*

-Life (and Death) Lessons from Xavier Hollow

Her ear-shattering scream had Xavier wincing, but he still latched onto Mercy's hand—her small, soft, and fragile hand—and tugged her to her feet. "You fall a lot."

That stopped her screaming. Her mouth hung open a moment, then she shook her head. "I'm not an angel."

"No." He took her in. Those tempting lips. Those perfectly curved breasts. The shapely hips. "You are not."

"But—but you just said—"

He let her go. Held up his hand and moved his thumb and index finger so that they were almost touching. "You got about that much angel pumping through you. You're a descendant. Pretty much human. Kinda a miracle that you exist, really. People like you tend to die young because the shine shows when you hit adulthood, and then the monsters hunt you, rip you apart, and then, boom...no more descendant."

The color left her cheeks. "I don't want to be ripped apart."

"Then you won't be." *Fuck.* Why had he just said that? He— "I won't let anyone rip you apart."

Her lashes fluttered. "Thank you."

Pain knifed through him. Truly, like a knife had just stabbed his foolish self right in the stomach. Then twisted. Why in the name of heaven and hell had he just vowed to protect her? He didn't protect anyone. He usually threw victims *to* the wolves, not the other way around. He didn't shield victims from attacks.

But she's mine.

No, no, no. No, no, no, no. He shook his head.

A little furrow appeared between Mercy's brows.

She's my victim. That's what I meant to think. My victim. "Usually, the offspring from an angel and human mating don't leave a big line behind them because they die before they can raise families. Your line must have been luckier than others."

Mercy swallowed. "It's...all true? What you're saying? Promise?"

He opened his hand and let his flames dance. "It's all true. Promise. Monsters are after you. They will be banging down the door any minute—"

Bang.

Bang.

Bang.

A wicked smile curved his lips. He was so in the mood to kick some ass. He'd hoped to start the day by fucking Mercy deliciously and slowly, but those plans had been altered, and he could really use the release of some violence. "Ah." Xavier tilted his head toward the banging on the door. "Someone arrived just as expected." He took a step toward the door.

Mercy grabbed his arm. "You don't know who is on the other side!"

The door trembled. It *would* be flying inward at any moment.

Mercy's hold tightened. "We should run."

Aghast, he gaped at her. "You're suggesting I *run* from my enemies? That I let them think they have more power than I do? Woman, do you know to whom you speak?" Outrage dripped from his words.

"Uh, Xavier. You said your name was—"

"*I* am the king of destruction." A reminder he shouldn't have to give. "I am immortal. I am power. I am death. I do not *run* from anyone or anything." His voice boomed as he added, "My enemies are the ones who run. But even retreat will not save them. If they seek to take what is mine, they will burn at my feet!"

Mercy blinked at him. "That was...a lot." She licked her lips. "It's sort of just...there's only one of you, and I don't know how many are at the door—*ah!*" Her words ended in a scream because the door had just flown open. It hurtled in the air, coming right for her.

Xavier turned and pulled her against his body. He shielded her, and the door slammed into his back. He grunted at the impact even as he felt the bones in his spine shatter. *Some bastard will pay for that.*

Being immortal didn't mean that he didn't feel pain. It didn't mean he couldn't be hurt. He could. He just didn't *die.*

It would normally take him a while to heal from injuries.

He didn't have a while.

He gripped her even as pain settled heavily around him like the old friend that it was. "Let me bite you." A quick infusion of her blood would have him healed in a flash.

"Do whatever you have to do," she cried back. "But I really hope I don't come in front of these bastards!"

Werewolves. They were the bastards in question. He could hear the growls behind him. Particularly ballsy bastards because normally the pack would never, ever hunt in the day. They couldn't shift fully when the sun was up. Yet they had still come out to attack...

They must want her very, very badly.

What they didn't seem to understand...was that he wanted her even more than they did.

He sank his teeth into Mercy's throat, and her blood—delicious, sweet, intoxicating—flowed over his tongue. She shuddered against him and let out a soft moan of pleasure, but he pulled away after only a few quick sips.

You will not come in front of these beasts. Her pleasure was his.

Power pulsed through him. Bones popped back into place, and he whirled to see his enemies.

Still in the form of men—just with claws and jagged teeth bursting from their mouths. Bigger than normal humans, probably closer to six foot seven or eight, with massive muscles.

Massive muscles and small-ass brains. Their brains had to be small, especially if they thought to take someone who belonged to him.

"Give...her..." A snarled order from the biggest of the beasts. The guy with shaggy, dirty brown hair and a shirt that looked as if it was a breath away from bursting at the seams.

Xavier heard Mercy whimper behind him. Why was she worried? He could take these— Xavier paused to count...*four, five, six*—he could take these six jerks in his sleep. He rolled his shoulders, straightened his already healed spine, and smiled. "She's mine. You'll have to take her over my cold, lifeless body."

Another whimper from Mercy, then she was digging her nails into his side. "No, absolutely not! Don't you dare go dying because of me!"

Preciously adorable. As if he would—*could*—die for anyone. Even if the task was possible, he certainly wouldn't do it. He'd never be a martyr. It was far, far better to be an executioner.

Xavier opened his palm and let his flames roll. "I'm trying to decide...should I let my fire turn you to ash or should *I* shift, and show you that being a pack of mangy dogs isn't that big of a deal? Not when I can turn into a dragon at a moment's notice."

The alpha—the one leading was always an alpha—gulped. "Y-You're Xavier..."

Clearly, he was.

"Xavier...about last night..."

"Last night. When you shifted and came at *me?*" he asked silkily. He wasn't surprised they knew who he was. All monsters should know. And tremble. With fear.

Then they should bow. Speaking of... Xavier frowned. "Why aren't you on your knees?"

"We didn't know it was you last night! Y-you aren't normally out in public—out with humans!" The alpha was still on his feet. Still not bowing. Silly werewolves. They always hated to show submission to someone else. Too bad for the alpha. A bit of submission *might* have saved his life.

"By the time we realized," the alpha added quickly, "you'd taken our prey and run!"

Xavier let his smile stretch and his flames dance higher. "Two mistakes. First, you should have recognized me on sight."

"You had on a mask!" One of the weaker wolves yelled.

Oh, the wolf did have a point. Xavier had forgotten that part. "I'm not wearing a mask now," he returned. "And yet you do not tremble before me. Instead, you seem intent on committing your *second* mistake yet again."

"Wh-what mistake is that?" From a blond wolf with lots of tats. Bad tats.

"Trying to take *my* prey."

Her nails dug deeper into his side. "Um, hate to interrupt," Mercy whispered. "But did you just call me prey?"

Yes, he had. "No one will take her from me. I'll let one—maybe two— of you live today so that you can spread the word and others will not make your same absolutely foolish and life-ending mistake."

The alpha looked back at his wolves. His claws stretched a wee bit more. Ah, someone was about to make mistake number three. Because the alpha wasn't going to order a retreat. He was going to order—

"*Attack!*" the alpha yelled. "Get the woman! We are going to rip her apart and drain every bit of magic that she—"

He died. Right there. Xavier's flames hit him and ignited the werewolf. He tried falling to the floor. Doing that stop, drop, and roll routine that humans used so often with fire. Perhaps that routine would have worked, if Xavier's fire had been normal. It wasn't. His flames were pure hellfire, and a bit of stopping, dropping, and rolling would not save anyone from his inferno.

Three seconds, and the alpha was ash.

The other werewolves froze.

"Who is next?" Xavier asked silkily.

Two wolves ran for the broken door. Xavier lifted both of his hands. Two balls of fire swirled and he got ready to send—

"*Don't kill them!*" Mercy locked her arms around his stomach. As if he wasn't just standing there with *fire* burning inches from his palms. "You can't just kill them!"

He let the flames fly. The two wolves who'd tried to retreat erupted when the balls hit them. "Of course, I can," he responded easily. "I just did. Do you not have a good view because you're mostly behind me?" Three wolves down. Three to go.

Who would be next?

Ah...you. A red-haired wolf let out a guttural scream and came at Xavier. Sighing, Xavier flicked his fingers and sent fire the werewolf's way. *Four down.* This fight was truly no challenge.

"Xavier, stop!" Mercy exclaimed. "You can't do this!"

He turned toward her. Locked his hands on her shoulders and saw her eyes go very, very wide...right before she looked at her shoulders, as if expecting to find herself on fire.

"I'm not planning to make you burn today," he told her.

She swallowed. "Thank...you?"

He grunted. "They wanted to use their claws to rip you apart. If I hadn't been here, they would have done so. They would have peeled the flesh from your skin. They would have sliced off your fingers and then your arms, and they would have carved open your chest—"

"I'm going to be sick," she gasped.

He let her go. Immediately.

She raced away. Presumably, to a bathroom. To be sick.

He didn't deal well with sick creatures. Humans or paranormals. So he turned back to his werewolf prey, half-expecting his two remaining enemies to have fled.

They hadn't. They were kneeling. With their heads bowed forward.

"We didn't know she was yours," one said. "I would never take what's yours."

The other—young, still wet behind the ears—peeked at Xavier. "You said...you said you'd let one or two of us live?"

Xavier crossed his arms over his chest. "I don't really need you both to live. One will do the trick." He looked back and forth between them. "Who shall be lucky? And who shall be dead?"

"Xavier!"

A long sigh came from him as he stiffened at Mercy's cry. "Shouldn't you be vomiting in a bathroom somewhere?"

"Don't kill them!" She rushed back to him. Reached out a hand to him. Stopped, because obviously, she was now terrified of him.

His eyes narrowed. *Scared of the monster before you?* If she was terrified in this moment, what would she be like when she saw him get really, really angry? When she saw the full force of his power? When she—

She reached out her hand and touched his wrist. Her touch sent heat—not fire, but a strange, soothing warmth—coursing through his veins. "You said two could go out and tell the world about me belonging to you."

Me belonging to you. He liked those words.

"Two can tell more people than just one. Two can cover twice as much ground. Talk to twice as many people." Her tongue swiped over her lower lip.

A drop of blood slid down her neck. Blood that had come from his bite.

His hand lifted. His fingers caught that drop of blood.

"Please." She trembled beneath his touch.

Fear.

For the first time in his very, very long life...

I don't like fear.

"Let them go," Mercy urged him. "I'm sure they will *promise* not to come after me again. No ripping me apart at all."

"They wouldn't dare touch you."

"Never!" From the two wolves. "We swear it!"

A wolf's vow was sacred. To break a vow would break the beast that a werewolf carried.

But Mercy wouldn't know that. She just stood there, trying to protect the beasts who would have killed her in an instant. "Why?" Xavier asked, truly confused. "Why do anything to help them?" Humans were always so hard to understand. Mercy's motivations seemed particularly difficult to decipher.

"Not them. I don't care about them." She shook her head. *"You* don't need more blood on your hands because of me. You don't have to kill for me. I didn't mean to ask you to do that. When I asked for protection, I-I didn't know the price you'd pay."

Killing people was as easy as breathing for him.

Sparing someone? It would hurt like a mother.

"Go," he thundered to the werewolves.

A knife seemed to sink into his gut. And twist. Over and over. *Fuck me. A good act never goes unpunished.*

"Tell the others!" Xavier snarled. "Make sure they all know...*no one touches her but me. Her shine belongs to me!*"

They ran.

Smart.

His gaze remained on Mercy. A Mercy who was paler than ghosts he'd seen before. A Mercy who trembled because she was terrified of him. But who...

Smiled at him. "Thank you," she murmured.

Stupid, ridiculous warmth spread through him and numbed his agony. Why? What was she doing to him?

He grabbed her hand. "You're coming with me."

She looked down at the ash that drifted across her floor. Mercy gulped. Then her gaze darted to the couch where Thomas still sprawled. Slowly, her gaze came back to Xavier.

"He lied to you. So did your stepfather. I've told you the truth." His thumb slid along her wrist. "Come with me?" A question. Deliberate. Because...

She has to give herself willingly.

Wasn't that the point of this whole curse? That he had to get her to give up everything for him?

Step one. *Give up her life in the human world.*

Mercy squared her shoulders. "Where will we go?"

"Someplace where other monsters can't get you."

She nodded. "Okay. Yes, yes, I'll come with you. You take me someplace safe..."

He'd take her to his world.

Heaven. Hell. After a while, it would seem the same to her.

He brought her hand to his mouth. His lips feathered over her knuckles. Xavier caught the flaring of her pupils. Despite everything she'd just seen, she was still aware of him.

Do you still want me?

Did she want him, in spite of her fear?

Or because of it?

He lowered her hand and leaned toward her. His mouth drew closer to hers—

"No." Her breath shuddered out as she shook her head. "Things are wild. Absolutely. But that dead man—"

"Werewolf, sweetheart. He was a werewolf. They're the ones with sharp teeth exploding from their mouths, muscles that look as if they've been on steroids for years, and glowing eyes."

A quick nod. "I'll remember that. But we can't kiss when a dead werewolf's ashes are blowing over my sneakers."

He smiled at her. "You have rules."

"I have rules."

"Then let's get the hell out of here." So that he *could* kiss her.

They turned for the door. Or the big hole where the door had been.

"Can you really shift into a dragon?" Mercy asked him.

He smiled. "I can shift into anything."

They stepped into the bright sunlight. An oddly pretty day. Xavier paused. Since when did he notice if days were pretty?

"Anything?"

Mercy's questioning voice had him glancing her way.

The sunlight hit her hair, catching the dark red highlights in the silky strands.

So much more than pretty.

"Anything," he assured her as he kept his hand twined with hers. The limo waited outside. Micah had arrived, as expected. He lounged near the back of the vehicle.

"Two got away!" Micah called, all cheerful. "Shall we hunt them down and rip out their insides?"

"I have better things to do." He stopped near Micah, but didn't enter the limo, not yet.

Micah's eyes widened. "Better than killing two werewolves?"

Xavier shrugged. "Take us to the Devil's Wishing Well."

And Micah's eyes widened even more. "You're taking her through? Already?"

Xavier thought the answer to that was obvious.

Micah's attention swept to Mercy. "You...you know what he is?"

"A monster," she said. Mercy bit her delectable lower lip. "Are you a monster, too?"

Micah opened his mouth—

"I'm sorry," Mercy rushed to add. "But you two don't seem like monsters at all. So you have...paranormal powers. I think you're more heroes than anything else. You keep saving me when I need help."

Had she just called him a hero? After he'd incinerated those jackass foes in front of her? As for Micah... "Close your mouth," Xavier ordered because Micah didn't need to gape that way. Then Xavier urged Mercy inside the limo.

She slipped in and didn't glance back.

Xavier paused and leaned in close to Micah. "Go in that house and get the drugs they were giving her. Find the entire pill bottle. I want to know exactly what those pills really are." A soft order. "Then take us to the Devil's Well." Plenty called it the Devil's *Wishing* Well. He preferred to just think of it as the Devil's Well.

A quick nod. "It hasn't even been twenty-four hours since the stroke of midnight! You are gonna have this in the bag! *She called us heroes!*"

"But, of course. What else would I be, if not the hero?" He ducked inside the limo.

The villain. That's what you are.

What he would always be.

But when Xavier got in the limo, Mercy was waiting for him. She'd crossed her legs, put her hands in her lap, and she stared at him with her wide, deep eyes.

The kind of eyes that dark witches used to steal a man's soul.

Only she was no witch.

Her shine was just as bright as ever.

"You can shift into anything?"

He slid beside her. Inhaled her peaches and cream scent. "You have an obsession with monsters, don't you?"

"Curiosity. I have a curiosity."

And that was why she was working to get a Ph.D. in monsters? Or mythology or whatever the hell she wanted to call her studies. Only the monsters she'd researched hadn't been real. Or, at least, most of them hadn't been real. "Yes, I can change into anything."

"Like...a puffer fish?"

He blinked at her. A...puffer fish? She had not said—no one would ever *dare* say to him—

"If you wanted, I mean, you could transform and become—"

He caught her chin and leaned in close. "Sweetheart, I'm no puffer fish." He stared into her eyes. She needed to understand this message. "I'm a fucking shark."

Then he kissed her.

Because there was no dead werewolf ash around her feet any longer.

Because they were alone in the back of the limo.

Because he wanted her.

And what he wanted, Xavier took.

CHAPTER SIX

*"Love? Hah. That's the ugliest lie of all.
If you fall for the lie, you're a fucking fool."*

-Life (and Death) Lessons from Xavier Hollow

Werewolves were real. They looked like huge bodybuilders with lots of sharp teeth.

Monsters were real. Lots of monsters.

And...Xavier had said he was some sort of king. *King of monsters?* He'd incinerated the wolves who'd said they were going to rip her apart.

He'd yanked back the veil blocking the world around her.

She should probably be running for her life. Maybe running and screaming. Truth be told, she'd almost fainted back at her house. But now...

Now she wasn't running. In fact, she was holding onto Xavier as tightly as she could. Holding him. Kissing him frantically. And, um, even crawling onto his lap and straddling him.

Slow down! A mental order.

But she didn't slow down. Because there was something about Xavier that seemed to send her body into overdrive. When he'd lightly bitten her after the wolves had blown in her door....

They huffed and puffed and blew my door down.

When his teeth had dipped into her skin, she'd felt a staggering surge of sensual hunger. Her body had yearned. Ached. She'd been on the precipice of a savage release again—

Then he'd let her go.

Put himself before her.

Fought for her.

Who said a monster can't keep you safe?

But other than the fire, he didn't look like a monster. He looked...he looked...*like the hottest fantasy I've ever had.* In a world that had told her she was mad, he was her sanity.

And the man could sure kiss.

A moan built in her throat. His hands clamped around her hips, and he hauled her against the thick, heavy length of his cock. He was aroused, no missing that. So was she. More aroused than she'd ever been in her entire life.

It wasn't natural. She knew it. Part of her was terrified. But part of her...part of her...

I don't want to let him go.

His mouth tore from hers, and she let out a quick cry of protest. But he just began to kiss a path down her throat. Her pulse pounded, and she knew he'd feel the frantic beat beneath his mouth. Was he going to bite her? When he bit her, she lost control. The pleasure took over.

She couldn't let go. She had to think, not just feel.

Dead werewolves.

"No!" She shoved against his shoulders.

The limo moved at the same time, and she would have fallen off his lap and hit the floor—she *did* start to fall—but his grip tightened, and he held her in place.

The sound of her ragged breathing filled the interior of the limo. His gaze locked on hers, and his eyes weren't dark. They were red.

"I should be so afraid of you," she said. The truth just came from her.

"You *are* afraid of me," his rumbling voice corrected her. "You just want me in spite of the fear. Don't worry, you aren't the first to feel that way."

Those words *hurt*. She flinched.

He frowned. "What happened to you?" His hands ran up her sides, then down her arms. Over the top of her legs. "What hurt you?" Anger roughened his voice.

"You did."

He lifted her up. Put her on the seat across from him in a flash. "I didn't summon my fire." He shook his head. "I didn't summon my fire," he said again as he lifted his hands and stared down at them. "I always have control."

"Your words."

His head whipped up.

"Your words hurt me."

His jaw locked. "Humans," he gritted out.

Yes, she was human. He wasn't. *Like that shouldn't have me running from the car.* But if she left him, she'd be on her own. With werewolves hunting her, alone wasn't a safe option. "I don't want to be part of some long line of women that fall at your feet." She fisted her hands. "Is it the bite? Do you always seduce your lovers with it?" Her eyes widened. "It's a vampire thing, isn't it? *Are* you a vampire?"

He stared back at her, and the red in his eyes slowly faded to darkness.

"Vampires, or some version of them, have been told in stories for thousands of years. Even Ancient Greeks and Romans had tales of blood drinkers." *He drank my blood, and I was okay with it. More than okay.* Meanwhile, whenever she gave blood during a blood drive, she nearly hit the floor. How did that make sense? "Almost every culture in the world has a creature that is similar to vampires." Inspiration struck. "Sekhmet!"

His eyes narrowed. "Excuse me?" Definite ice entered his voice.

Her head tilted as Mercy studied him. She saw no sign of his fangs. Could he make them appear and disappear at will? "Sekhmet was an Egyptian warrior goddess—linked to both healing and the plague." Talk about two opposites. "But some scholars happen to think she was the oldest vampire to ever exist. The first one."

"Not likely," Xavier muttered. "And you *do* know how to kill a mood, don't you?"

He was the one who had actually *killed* less than ten minutes ago. Mercy huffed out a breath. "She was sent to punish humans, only she couldn't stop drinking their blood. She was also said to have the breath of fire." And Xavier was sure handy at tossing flames.

Xavier settled back against the leather seat. "You think I'm some fire-breathing vampire?"

Well, it was a possibility.

"Insulting." He sniffed. "Do more, monster researcher. Do better. I told you already, I am the king of destruction. I control fire. I shift into any beast I want. And I can drink blood, sure, but I'm not just *drinking* your blood. When I drink, I take power from my prey."

Prey. Goosebumps rose onto her arms. "Am I prey?"

He blinked. "Circumstances with you are unusual. I had to drink from you after the ball because your idiot human friend—the man you should have let me kill, by the way—shot me. I heal faster with an injection of magic. Same situation happened in your home. When the door hit me—as I was bravely using my body to protect you—my spine shattered in multiple places. If I hadn't bitten you, I would have fallen into a puddle and been utterly useless to you as the werewolves ripped you apart right in front of me." He waved his left hand vaguely toward her. "But, no, do go on about how I'm barely better than an Egyptian goddess who got blood drunk and nearly eradicated her own people."

"Your spine shattered?" She reached out and her hand touched his knee. "That happened to you because of me?"

His gaze dipped to her hand.

"I'm sorry," she said, meaning those words. "The last thing I want is for you to hurt."

His stare rose. Pinned her. "Truly?"

"Of course. I don't particularly want anyone to hurt." *Don't think about the dead werewolves. Don't.*

He smiled. The slow, stretching smile lit the darkness of Xavier's eyes and stole her breath. "You have a kind heart."

Her hand left his leg and rose to press over her heart because that smile of his made it ache.

"It will probably be the death of you," he added. His smile had vanished.

She couldn't look away from him. "How do I get the monsters to stop hunting me?"

"You have to lose the shine that brings them to you."

"They didn't come before. I-I've always had the shine?" Had she? Mercy had no clue. "They didn't come for me until last night." A sudden thought pierced her. "The same time you came for me."

"The shine probably first appeared when you were around eighteen. Maybe a little older. That's what it usually does. That would have been close to the time when your mother was killed in front of you." He stopped. Frowned. "I'm...sorry for your loss." Xavier winced. "Fuck, that hurt."

"What did?"

"Nothing." His nostrils flared. "Sorry you had to see her die."

Even as he'd said the word *sorry*, he'd hissed out a hard breath, as if he'd just taken a punch.

"What is happening with you?" Her head cocked. "You seem to be in pain." Mercy sucked in a quick breath as worry pierced her. "Are you sure your spine healed?"

"I'm fine." Bit off.

He sounded anything but fine.

"Your shine couldn't have been apparent when your mother died or you would have been slaughtered with her."

A flinch. That had certainly been a brutal statement. But, probably true.

"Then your stepfather and his minion started you on the pills. I'm thinking the pills dulled your shine." A pause as the car kept sliding through town. "How long ago did you stop taking the pills?"

"I haven't stopped." Not really. "Yesterday? Today. I definitely haven't had one today."

"Has to be longer than that. My man saw you days ago."

Her eyes widened. "You...wait. Back up. Someone who works for you saw me?"

His hand scraped over his hard jaw. "I knew you'd be the target of individuals with ill intent. Figured you needed someone stronger to keep them away from you. I got to you as soon as I could."

Oh. That had been kind. *Something a hero does, not a monster.* "Without you, I'd be dead."

"Yes."

"Thank you." And she leapt across the limo again. Not to give him some passionate kiss, but to hug him. Life mattered. That this man—this stranger—had risked so much overwhelmed her.

He might call himself a monster, but he wasn't. He was her savior.

His hands pressed lightly to her waist. "What are you doing?"

"Hugging you." Probably too hard. She should ease up. She didn't. Not yet. She inhaled his scent and enjoyed the warmth and strength of him.

"Why? Why are you embracing me? This doesn't feel like a sexual embrace."

Her head whipped up. She almost clipped him on the chin. "It's...uh, not."

"Pity."

She should get back across the limo. But she didn't. "Hasn't anyone ever given you a hug before? One that is just about—about caring? Or about being grateful? I'm grateful to you. I appreciate you."

He stiffened. "Can't you just want to fuck me?"

"I want to do that, too." Total truth. Why lie to him? Especially since she seemed to be living on borrowed time. "But I also just want to hug you." So she did it, again.

He curled around her and...hugged her back.

"Pleasant enough," he muttered. "But fucking is still better."

Mercy smothered a smile. "I'm sure it probably is."

"You're...*probably* sure?"

Don't stop your confessions now. She tucked her head against his shoulder. "I've never had sex, so I can't really speak from experience. I got close a few times but..."

She was across the limo. In her seat. He knelt on the floorboard before her. His hands were like steel bands around her waist.

"Virgin," he growled. "Virgin with *angel* blood."

Mercy cleared her throat. "Mercy," she corrected him. "I think I like that title way better. And let's not be weird about this. Guys always get weird. Some of them immediately run away when they find out I haven't had sex before. Others seem to see me as a challenge. I'm not a prude or a challenge. I just...it's hard when you think you're hallucinating. When you're afraid you could lose your grasp on reality at any moment." *Because there are monsters everywhere.* "It's hard to trust someone. Not like I wanted to go falling for the bad guy."

His hands jerked from her body. "Absolutely. Wouldn't want that. How horrible would that be for you."

The car door opened.

When had they stopped?

A startled gasp came from that open door. Then, *"My king?"* Stunned. "Are you...are you kneeling?"

"Fuck," Xavier rumbled. "She's a virgin."

Her hand flew to cover his mouth.

He blinked at her.

"That is not news we share with the world," she told him as her cheeks flamed. Her voice was barely a breath of sound. "That is intimate information that is just for me and for you. For us alone, understand?"

She felt the sensual glide of his tongue against her palm. As if he'd burned her—which she hoped he would never, ever do—her hand whipped back.

He sent her a wicked grin. "I like things for us alone."

And I like that grin of his too much.

Before she could think of a response, he'd exited the vehicle. Mercy took a moment to suck in a deep breath and to very much hope that the red flush would leave her cheeks.

"That makes her even more valuable," Micah said.

That just pissed her off. Mercy bolted from the limo. She pointed at Micah as he huddled with Xavier. "Being a virgin or not being a virgin has zero to do with my value. How dare you say otherwise?"

Micah took three fast steps away from her. His wide eyes were on her pointing finger. Then he exhaled. "Whoa. For a moment there, I was afraid she'd shoot fire, too."

She felt like shooting some fire.

He lifted his hands in surrender. "I meant the beasts hunting you would find that valuable. They get more of a rush from destroying innocence. It's a monster thing."

A monster thing. How fabulous.

"You should ditch the virginity at the first chance," Micah told her with a quick nod. "It will make you less of a target to them. And if they know you belong to Xavier, they'll be pissing themselves with fear and won't look as hard for you."

Ditch it at the first chance?

"Micah, shut the hell up," Xavier advised him.

His mouth clamped closed. But his gleaming eyes said...*Ditch it.*

"Get rid of the limo," Xavier added flatly. "I'll see you back at the castle."

Micah rushed to the front of the car.

"Castle?" Mercy latched onto that one word. "As in fairytales and princesses?" That vibe didn't go with what she knew of Xavier.

"As in dungeons and torture rooms." He offered his arm to her. "Shall we dine first?"

Dungeons and torture rooms definitely fit him better. She took his offered arm and looked around. Hold on. She knew this place. She'd come to the restaurant for brunch before. Big, dark and elaborate wrought-iron gates waited just a few feet away. *Charm gates.* That was what she'd been told by an employee when she visited previously. With her particular area of academic interest, there was no way she could have been in New Orleans and not visited this restaurant.

The gates had supposedly been made by Queen Isabella of Spain. As Mercy and Xavier passed them, her left hand reached out to trail over one gate. "Charm," she murmured. That was the legend. The gates had been blessed so that if you touched them, you could get a little of that charm yourself.

I could use some charm right about now.

A staff member jumped to attention at the sight of Xavier and ushered them into the beautiful courtyard. At this time of the day, she expected to see a crowd, but the courtyard was empty. Birds chirped overhead and when she looked up, Mercy saw the twisting vines and the hanging lights that blocked out most of the sun from reaching the area.

They were seated right in front of an old, stone wishing well. The waitress rushed away, glancing back once or twice with a worried look on her pretty face.

"Why is no one else out here?" Mercy asked, leaning forward.

Xavier shrugged. "Because I didn't want them to be."

"You arranged this?"

"Micah helped. He's excellent at taking care of details." He reached for the glass of water that had been left on the table for him. "Micah...didn't mean to upset you." Halting. "He gets so focused on helping me that he forgets about others."

"Because you're his king?" *A king who lives in a castle and can shift into anything and can shoot fire from his fingertips.*

Beneath the table, she reached down and pinched her thigh, just in case. Nope, still not dreaming.

"Because I am his king." He put down the water. His head turned away as he stared at a nearby fountain. Water trickled down in a soothing melody. The fountain looked new. Modern. Beautiful. A stark contrast to the old well.

After a moment, Xavier continued, "Micah serves me so well because I am his king and because I spared him a long time ago."

Three staff members bustled out. They came with trays of food that they put on the table with nervous hands. Mercy thanked them before they nearly ran away, then she frowned at Xavier. "I thought there was a buffet inside?" The last time she'd been at the restaurant, everyone had been eating at a scrumptious buffet.

"Not for us." He picked up a fork.

The delicious scents from the food teased her nose. *I'm having brunch with the king of destruction.* "Seems strange for someone like you to just be having a meal." The food smelled too good. She couldn't resist any longer. Mercy reached for a fluffy biscuit. And some blackberry jelly.

He dove into the shrimp and grits. "Monsters eat. We drink. We fuck."

She nearly choked on her biscuit. "Of...course."

They ate in silence. Or at least, they ate until she had to blurt, "How did you spare him?"

Xavier paused in the act of using a napkin to dot his mouth.

"Micah. How did you spare him?"

"Micah is supposed to be a werewolf. His family created the fiercest pack the world has ever seen. His father was a truly bloodthirsty bastard who would cut down his enemies with zero hesitation." What could have been an admiring sigh slipped from him. "Then Micah was born. Weak. The whelp of the pack. That pack hates weakness of any kind. Remember how the Spartan soldiers would get rid of any child that showed infirmity? Because they were imperfect?"

She nodded.

"In his father's eyes, Micah was imperfect. No supernatural strength. And when he shifted, he'd get stuck. A half-man, half-beast whelp that couldn't attack anyone. He was cast out, left to die...left to be hunted. Hunted by his own kind. His father even made Micah's death into a game for the pack. Whoever brought back his head first was going to get a big reward."

She couldn't eat anything else. Her knife clattered onto the plate. "That's horrible."

"That's life."

A callous response and yet...Mercy leaned forward. "Micah doesn't look dead to me."

Xavier's gaze sharpened on her. "Appearances can be deceiving. That's an important lesson." He stroked his chin. "You know, I always thought I should write a life lesson manual for mortals. They make such foolish mistakes all the damn time."

"Yes, maybe you should do that. Excellent plan. Genius."

Was it her imagination, or did he preen a little bit?

She cleared her throat. "And are you saying *I'm* making a foolish mistake?"

"You're trusting me. You shouldn't be." A pain-filled hiss escaped him.

Mercy caught herself leaning toward him. "If you were truly evil, why would you warn me away from you?" Didn't make sense at all to her. Something else that didn't make sense? "What's up with the random sounds of pain you make?" Like the little hiss that he'd just given. "Is something wrong?" *Don't ask. Don't.* But... "Xavier, is something wrong with you?" The darkest, scariest thought... "Are you dying?"

His expression had turned completely unreadable. "Would you care?"

"Yes." Her instant response.

"Excellent." A smile that flashed a lot of white teeth, but, fortunately, no fangs. "As for what's wrong with me, I'm allergic to being good."

She laughed.

He didn't.

Her hands grabbed for her glass. She downed a few massive swallows of water. Then managed, "Say it again?"

"Being *good*," he shuddered, "even in small ways causes me pain. 'No good deed goes unpunished.' I'm sure you've heard the saying. It was literally made for me."

She wanted to laugh again, but couldn't. Instead, she managed, "You're not serious."

"As a heart attack."

The birds kept chirping. He motioned around them. "This place is supposed to be magical. If you see movement from the corner of your eye, it could be a sprite. They like to steal things so be careful."

"I don't have anything to steal," she said, feeling dazed. *He's allergic to being good.*

"Sure you do. That shine is so bright it glows around you."

He kept talking about her shine. She had the feeling he was trying to distract her. Too bad. Mercy wasn't in the mood to be distracted. "You've protected me. That's something *good.*"

"Yes."

She kept attempting to put together the puzzle that was Xavier. "It hurt you to protect me."

He rolled one shoulder. "It is what it is."

Aghast, she could only shake her head. "I don't want you hurting for me."

He rose and walked around the table. Xavier towered over her as he blocked out the few rays of sunlight that had managed to trickle past the vines that hung overhead. His hand lifted and skimmed down her cheek. He seemed to like touching her that way. The skim of his knuckles over her cheek.

She liked it when he touched her that way, too.

"It's not a big deal," he muttered. "Sometimes, it's just a bit of hives."

She'd seen him scratching his shoulder a few—

"Other times, it's like a knife to my gut. One that someone drives into me and twists for the hell of it."

That was awful. Mercy had to blink away tears because he'd been hurt by trying to do something *nice.*

"But if the act is big enough, it will be like having all the skin ripped from my body. Do something too good, and even the king of destruction will die." Surprise flashed on his face. "I shouldn't have told you that. I haven't...no one knows that but me."

And now me.

He started to back away. Her hand flew up and curled around his wrist. "Stop being good." A tear leaked down her cheek.

His eyes narrowed. "Excuse me?"

"Be bad. Don't do anything else that will get you hurt." His pain wasn't an option. His death?

Could not happen. "Be as bad as you can possibly be."

He leaned toward her. His mouth came temptingly close. "I shall be."

Her head tipped back because she wanted his mouth on her. She wanted him. More than she'd ever wanted anyone before. Beyond reason and sanity, she craved him.

Because of the bite?

Because he was someone bad who'd been good...for her?

Or because...*he's Xavier*?

"Are you crying for me?"

She was. Dammit.

He caught the teardrop on her cheek. "Precious," he rasped. He brought his index finger—and that teardrop to his mouth. His eyes closed as he seemed to *taste* her tear. "Humans don't cry for me."

"I just did. I am."

His eyes opened. "I don't like the taste of your pain."

Once more, she blinked away the tears. She would not let more fall. "If you don't like it, then don't do anything else that will make me cry. Stop being good."

"I don't think you'd like me bad."

"I like you just fine as you are."

He leaned in ever closer. His mouth hovered over hers. "You don't know what I'm really like."

Yes, she did. He was the monster who was enduring pain for her. *Not a monster.* Her hero. "Kiss me," she whispered.

He did. Not roughly. Not with fury. Softly. Carefully. As if she was something precious and he wanted to savor her. With careful seduction and banked need. With the skill of a gentleman and the charm of a lover holding himself back.

"No," she softly commanded against his mouth. "No more being good. Be *you*."

Instantly, the kiss changed. Harder. Deeper. So much more demanding. His tongue plunged past her lips as he took and claimed. Possession and savage desire.

She rose from the chair. He pulled her against him. The hard press of his cock was undeniable as her body brushed against his. He kissed her with a drugging hunger that made passion pulse through her body.

She wanted their clothes gone.

Wanted everything gone...The danger. The restaurant. The rules of society that said she shouldn't throw caution to the wind with a man she'd just met.

She wanted all the doubts gone.

She just wanted *him*. The pleasure he offered.

No fear. No regret.

Pleasure.

She could almost hear the seductive whisper in the air around her.

His mouth lifted from hers. "You come to my world, and the others won't follow you."

She wanted his mouth again. "H-how do I get there?"

He let her go. Primitive desire tightened his face. "You see that well?"

Hard to miss it. She'd asked about the well on her first visit. "The Devil's Wishing Well."

"So legend says." He opened his hand, and a gleaming, silver coin rested in his palm. "You toss this coin into the well, and you make a wish."

Light hit the coin, making it gleam even more. "What wish do I make?"

"You wish to be my...companion in another world."

"Companion?"

He reached for her hand. Tucked the coin against her palm. It felt so warm. Not hot. Just warm.

"Wish for me to take you away. Wish it. Toss in the coin, and I can transport you to another place. The monsters there are all under my command. An army to keep you shielded from those others hunting you."

She looked at the well. "You won't be hurt. There—in that world—you don't have to do anything else...good. You can be—"

"Bad?" Xavier finished, voice very, very careful. "If that's what you want me to be."

Her feet shuffled toward the well. Their table had been positioned right in front of the well. Heavy bricks formed the bottom of the well, and a white, wrought-iron arch curled around the top. A small bucket on a metal chain hung from that arch.

She looked down into the well. "I can't see the bottom."

"That's because I'm with you. For everyone else, it will just be a well. A spot for tourists to see. For you, it will be so much more."

Her head turned toward him.

"There's old magic here, so this place can be a gateway for you. Humans can only enter my world through gateways like this one. And you need to pay the right price."

The coin still felt warm. The way he felt warm against her. "I just drop it in and make a wish?"

"That's all." He stalked closer. "Well, there is *one* more thing."

Her stomach knotted. "I was afraid of that."

"You have to jump in the well."

"Excuse me?"

"Jump. In. But don't worry. I'll be there to catch you when you land."

"You'd better be," she muttered. Okay, this was it. Her hand extended. Her eyes closed.

"Wish for me to take you away." His breath fluttered over her cheek.

I wish—

Her fingers began to unfurl.

Something hard grabbed her wrist. "Not so fast." A rumbling, male voice.

Her eyes flew open. Her head jerked to the right, toward that voice. A man with thick, blond hair and the face of—of an angel smiled at her.

"Haven't you heard...?" The stranger kept holding her wrist. "It's dangerous to trust the devil."

CHAPTER SEVEN

*"Fate loves to fuck with you. Think you've got
total control? That's freaking hilarious."*

-Life (and Death) Lessons from Xavier Hollow

He'd been so close. So damn close! Wind
whipped into the courtyard as Xavier's fury
spilled past his control. "Get your hand *off* her,
brother!" A low, lethal snarl. "If you don't, I'll cut
it off."

Mercy's head whipped toward Xavier. "Did
you just say this guy is your brother?"

"One of many." All of them were colossal
pains in his ass. And Paxton hadn't let go of
Mercy. Xavier let claws burst from his fingertips,
and he slashed down with his hand at his
brother's wrist.

Before he lost his hand, Paxton released
Mercy and jumped back. "You could have hurt
her! What if your claws had cut her instead of
me?" He made a *tsk* sound as he shot a
sympathetic glance Mercy's way. "Do you see
what a beast you have, my dear? And you were

about to give your life to him! It's so fortunate for you that I arrived when I did."

How about *unfortunate?* Xavier pulled Mercy behind him. The better to shield her from Paxton's BS. "What the hell are you doing here?"

Paxton smiled. It was his innocent, charming smile. The one that made him look extra harmless but actually meant he was at his most devious. "I went to a lovely, little ball last night. Traffic delayed me a bit so I arrived a wee bit tardy." He lifted his hand and *snapped* his fingers. "We can't all just *snap* about."

"Still resent that, huh?" Xavier taunted. "Tough shit."

His brother sniffed. "Imagine my surprise when I found blood-stained angel wings in the alley behind the building. And that blood I discovered? I couldn't help but notice that it carried your stench, Xavier."

"The world is just full of incredible surprises." Xavier felt Mercy's fingers flutter on his back. *Paxton should not be here.* "You're not allowed in this space. It's mine. You're violating our treaty."

"Don't go getting so territorial and growly. Makes you seem like a beast."

Oh, I will show you a beast.

Paxton rolled one shoulder as if he had no cares in the world. He typically didn't. "Calm yourself. I'm only here for a brief visit. Just came to save the damsel from making a terrible mistake." He craned to see around Xavier. "Hello, damsel."

"I'm *not* a damsel," Mercy snapped.

"Oh, are you not?" Paxton hummed, then added, "A lovely woman. In obvious distress. One who is being misled by a monster. Seems like a damsel to me." Again with the *tsk* sound that grated like nails on a chalkboard. "You can't trust Xavier. Despite what he's told you, my brother isn't here to save you. He can't. He was born to destroy."

That was Paxton's big bombshell? Xavier laughed. He also stepped to the right, moving so that Mercy was at his side instead of behind him. For this part, he wanted them to be a united front. He caught her hand and brought it to his lips. A quick glance reassured him that her other hand remained closed over *his* coin. "Mercy knows what I am." Did he sound proud? He kinda was. She knew exactly what he was, and she'd still been ready to leap for him.

She'll sacrifice herself for me.

"This lovely human knows you're the king of destruction?" A sly smile curled Paxton's lips. His blue eyes gleamed. The asshole always managed to look so innocent.

But then, he should. That particular trick was part of his least favorite brother's power. Damn annoying.

"Xavier told me about that already," Mercy replied without missing a beat. She inched closer to Xavier's side. "So who are *you*?"

Paxton bent and offered her a graceful bow. "The king of dreams, at your command."

Mercy frowned at Xavier. "How many kings are running around New Orleans?"

"Seven," Paxton said as he straightened. "Well, not all of us are in New Orleans. We're out and about in lots of places. And seven is just the brothers. Don't get me started on our sisters." He shuddered.

Mercy shook her head. "I don't understand."

"That's because *he's* lying to you," Xavier told her. A little furrow had appeared between her brows. *Pax, you are messing things up for me. I almost had her.* "He isn't the king of dreams. Paxton is the king of illusions."

Soft laughter escaped from Paxton. "Ah, but what is a dream...if not the sweetest illusion of all?" His gaze drifted over Mercy. Lingered on her chest—near her heart.

Xavier knew the prick wasn't focusing on Mercy's gorgeous breasts. No, instead, Paxton was busy looking at—

"Such a beautiful shine," Paxton murmured.

Xavier stiffened. "Get the fuck away from her, or I will kill you where you stand."

More laughter. "You think you can? In a few days' time, you won't be killing anyone. I, on the other hand, won't have that problem."

Mercy bumped into Xavier's side. "What does he mean?"

"Don't believe what he says," Xavier warned her. "Illusions are lies. Since illusions are his bread and butter, that means he's the king of illusions *and* lies."

"Oh." She nodded. Her head tilted as she studied Paxton. "So what is it that you are allergic to?"

Paxton took a step back. "Excuse me?"

"What makes you hurt? If Xavier is the king of destruction, then he's supposed to rip things apart. When he's good and puts them together, it hurts him." Her hair slid over her shoulder. "You're about illusion and lies. So I'm guessing the opposite hurts you. Is it truth? Is that what brings you pain?"

Paxton took another step back. His accusing stare swung to Xavier. "You told her my weakness?" What could have been fear—maybe even some betrayal, too—flashed on his face.

But his brother needed to settle down. Xavier hadn't spilled any deep, dark family secrets. "No. She just happens to be an expert on monsters. Guess she's good at figuring us out."

"You will regret this!" Paxton raged.

Like he needed to deal with Paxton's drama. "Yeah, I'm so over this scene. You've outstayed your welcome. Bye, brother." Xavier summoned fire and hurtled it at his brother.

Paxton went running. For now.

Xavier urged Mercy back to the well. "Make the wish," he ordered her. "Now." Before Paxton came back with reinforcements.

He would. He always did. The dick.

Her lashes fluttered. "I'm...going to be safe with you?" Her hand extended over the well.

A lump rose in his throat. Xavier choked it down. "Do you trust me?" *Don't. You shouldn't. I am not the man you should trust.*

He wasn't a man at all.

Monster.

But if she stayed there and Paxton came back...

Xavier looked over his shoulder. Already, the edges of the restaurant's walls had begun to twist and churn. From the growing darkness, he could see snakes slithering toward them. *Illusions.* But some illusions could scare you to death.

"I trust you." She dropped the coin into the well. "I wish you'd take me away."

She climbed onto the edge of the well. And then she stepped over the edge. Just in time. A striking snake lunged for her, but it missed as Mercy fell.

***

A scream built in her throat because Mercy just kept falling and falling and there was nothing but darkness around her. A complete and total darkness that seemed to surround her and suffocate her. Mercy had the terrible feeling that she was falling straight into hell. She couldn't hold back the terror for even another second. *"No! Help me—"*

She landed. In his arms.

"Got you," Xavier told her cheerfully.

The darkness vanished as a circle of flames surrounded them. She looped her arm over the back of his neck and gasped as she tried to choke down her fear.

"That wasn't so bad, was it?" Xavier sent her his wicked smile.

"It was horrible," she told him truthfully because she liked being truthful with him. He was the first person—er, supernatural being?—who knew all her secrets and her fears. "I thought I was dying—or going to hell—and that I would never stop falling."

His smile faded. As did the flames around them. "I told you that I would catch you. I always will when you fall for me."

She swallowed and managed to haul her gaze off Xavier and to actually look around. When she did, her breath left her in a quick rush.

She was in the most beautiful room she'd ever seen. Gleaming walls. *Golden* light that seemed to spill from everywhere. And when she looked up...wow. It looked as if she was staring straight at a million sparkling stars. Real stars, not the little fake ones that she'd put up in her bedroom when she'd been a kid. Those stars had glowed at night for her, and the glow had helped her to push away her fears.

Fears of monsters.

Because she'd always feared them. Not just when her mother had died. *Always.*

His hold tightened on her. "You are safe here." He carried her toward the bed. A beautiful bed that hung from ropes that were attached to that magical, star-filled ceiling. "You should rest some." He lowered her onto the bed. It swayed lightly beneath her. "Going through dimensions can take a lot out of humans."

She felt shaky, yes. On edge. And her heart kept racing.

Xavier started to back away from the bed. From her. Mercy grabbed his hand.

He stilled. Then looked at her fingers as they curled around his wrist.

"It's like the biggest adrenaline rush of my life," she whispered. "I feel energy pouring through every cell in my body."

A muscle flexed along his jaw. "That will go away, soon enough."

Her lips had become desert dry, so she wet them, then asked, "Did it go away soon for the other humans you brought here?"

"These are my chambers. You are the first I have ever brought here."

That mattered. It *had* to matter, didn't it?

"Get some sleep," he urged her. "We'll talk more when you wake up." Xavier pulled away from her and strode for the door.

She missed him instantly. "I trust you."

He stilled.

She rose onto her knees. The bed swayed. Okay, that swaying would take a little getting used to. "I don't care what your brother said. I hardly think you're the devil."

He glanced back at her. "No, I'm not. Most people said that was my father."

What? She felt her mouth drop open.

His eyes gleamed. "Scared of me now?"

"Are you—are you teasing me?"

After a careful beat of time, Xavier turned to fully face her. "No. I'm truly asking if you are scared of me."

So much light spilled into that chamber. But...Her eyes narrowed. The light seemed to stop when it neared Xavier. In fact, she could just make out a few shadows clinging to him. Like the shadows that she used to see around the monsters she'd feared so much. Her breath caught.

"I thought so." Flat words from him. "Guess that last revelation was a little too much for you, wasn't it? I'm the king of destruction, one of the many sons of the devil, and you are in my world now where you will be—"

She jumped off the bed. Managed not to fall, thankfully. A win. And Mercy bounded toward him. Those shadows around him reached out to her, but she ignored them and the odd chill that wanted to rise on her skin. Her hands closed around his arms. Went *through* those shadows so she could touch him. He felt steel hard beneath her touch.

"What are you doing?" he rasped.

"There are shadows around you," she whispered.

"They've always been there." Grim. "Always will be." But his gaze had narrowed on her. "Only you see them now? When you didn't before?"

She nodded. "I see them." Once, shadows like the ones clinging to him would have sent her running. Or, at the very least, they would have made Mercy think she was crazy.

"Maybe the pills really are wearing out of your system. Or maybe whatever your stepfather gave you just doesn't work in my world." His lips twisted. "Either way, I guess you see me for what I am now, don't you?" His fangs appeared behind his twisted smile, and his eyes began to burn red.

Mercy didn't let him go. "Yes, I see you for what you are." She would not back down. Her whole body felt jittery. Too warm. Too shaken. Too...everything. Everything in her life had turned topsy-turvy. Everything was out of control, including her. But one thing remained solid.

Xavier.

Back at the wishing well, he'd stepped in front of her when he thought his brother was a threat.

At her house, he'd taken down the werewolves for her.

At the ball, he'd been shot because he jumped before a bullet that had been coming her way.

He was no monster.

She'd asked him to kiss her before. This time, she didn't ask. Mercy shot onto her toes even as her hands hauled him toward her. It was probably his surprise more than anything else that had him surging down toward her.

And she put her mouth on his. She kissed him wildly. Frantically, passionately. She kissed Xavier as if he was the only thing in her world that mattered.

Because in that moment, he was.

His hands clamped around her waist. He lifted her up against him with an easy strength that probably should have frightened her, but she was past the point of being afraid of any part of him. This was her Xavier. So when he lifted her up, she just wrapped her legs around his waist and held on. She opened her mouth wider. And she kissed him even more passionately. His taste had her craving him desperately. His touch seemed to brand her through her clothing. She arched and rubbed her hips against him, over and over, needing more than what she had. Mercy wanted their clothes gone. She wanted to be skin to skin with him.

No, she wanted him in her. As deep in her as he could go.

But his head lifted. Xavier took that wicked, skillful mouth of his from her. His breath heaved as he stared into her eyes. "Why?"

"Why...what?"

"Why are you kissing me when you should be running?"

"Because I only want to run to you." Didn't he see that? "Because I feel safe—truly safe—for the first time in my life when I'm with you."

His thick lashes flickered. Xavier began to shake his head.

So she told him, "You keep the monsters at bay."

"I *am* the monster."

"No, no, you're not." She kissed him again. Held him tighter. "You are so much more," Mercy said against his mouth.

But he was walking. Still holding her. But walking. And—

He let her go. Dropped her onto the bed.

She sprawled on the mattress as it swayed lightly, and Mercy stared up at him.

"I am a monster. You need to see that." His eyes burned so red.

Fine. Her chin lifted. If he insisted on calling himself a monster... "Then you're my monster."

He lunged toward her. Caught himself. "You need to be *sure*."

"I am sure of you. I'm also sure that it's past time for me to stop being a virgin. Tick, tock, Xavier."

That muscle jerked in his jaw again. "It's...because of what Micah said," he gritted out.

"This has nothing to do with Micah." She hauled her shirt over her head and tossed it aside. She also kicked off her sneakers and shimmied out of her jeans. It was exceptionally hard and awkward to shimmy when the bed was moving, but she accomplished the task and was soon only in her panties and bra. The virginal white ones. "It's because I have been waiting for you."

His nostrils flared.

"Have you been waiting for me?" Mercy asked him. He hadn't, of course, and she shouldn't have posed that question. Just because he felt right to her, just because she looked into his eyes and thought...*There you are*...none of that meant he felt the same way about her.

"All my life," he said, and there was a ring of truth to his words that she couldn't ignore.

She reached out to him.

Xavier crashed onto her. He came down onto the bed hard and fast, and if she thought they'd been swaying before, it was nothing to the way they *soared* now. The bed seemed to fly across the room, only to surge back, and a startled cry escaped her.

He swallowed her cry and kissed her until she didn't give a damn about what the bed was doing. All she cared about was him.

Deeper, hungrier, he kissed her.

His hands flew over her body. The bra and panties seemed to vanish. Truly, vanish. As did his clothes because she could feel his powerful body against hers, and there was no longer anything between them.

He positioned her on the bed. Spread her out beneath him, and when she tried to grab for him because she was greedy to touch every inch of his body, Xavier caught her hands and pinned them above her head.

Her breath sawed out as she stared up at him. He looked big, dangerous, and so sexy that she was getting wet just from staring at him.

Then he smiled...

Her sex clenched.

"I am going to taste every single inch of you."

Yes, fabulous. Go for that.

"And you're not going to move. You're going to let me have my wicked way with you, aren't you, my Mercy?"

"Only if you let me have my wicked way with you."

He blinked. Then, if possible, he looked even hungrier. "Always."

She started to smile. But stopped because he'd just shoved her thighs even wider apart as he lowered between them. His mouth went right to her core. She'd thought there would be preliminaries. That he would work up to the next part. He didn't.

He drove his tongue into her.

There was no working up to anything.

His tongue and his lips and his fingers took her, and there was no way she could not move. She *had* to move. Her body twisted and surged and arched and shuddered.

"Naughty Mercy," he breathed against her, and she felt his fingers stroking her clit right before his tongue licked her feverishly. "Am I gonna have to punish you for breaking the rules?" Another lick. More. Faster and faster. He was licking her clit and thrusting his fingers into her and Mercy was helpless. No other word.

Helpless.

Helpless against the onslaught of need. Against the brutal, seductive skill of his mouth. Against the climax that crashed over her and all she could do was scream out his name as she came for him.

And Xavier lapped her up. Seemed to drink up every bit of her pleasure, and it just enflamed him more because he kept tasting and taking and the first orgasm didn't even get a chance to fully end before she was barreling into another. Too fast and hard and her whole body quaked. "Xavier!" She grabbed for him, and her nails raked over his shoulders. *"You."* Desperate. Maddened. "I want *you* in me."

This wasn't what a first time was supposed to be like. She got that. First times...they were awkward. Fumbled. Quick. Or at least, that was what her friends had said. *Have an orgasm your first time? Yeah, right, good luck with that.*

Clearly, her friends had never fucked a self-proclaimed monster. It was the way to go.

Because her first time...it was frantic. Consuming. Mind-shattering.

He looked up at her. Licked his lips as if he still tasted her.

Oh, wow.

His stare ate her alive. So much burning fire. And his fangs were even longer. How had he managed not to nip her with them?

And what would it feel like if he did? Would she feel that insane surge of pleasure from his bite again?

"Xavier..." Softer.

"You are mine." He rose above her. Put the wide head of his cock against her. But didn't sink in.

What was he waiting for? Christmas?

Her legs locked around his hips. Her heels dug into his ass. "And you're mine."

His eyes widened.

He sank deep.

There was the smallest flash of pain. There one second, gone the next, and all she knew after that flash was pleasure. Pleasure coursing through her veins. Filling every cell of her body. She thrashed beneath him, and he caught her hands once again. He pushed them down against the mattress. The mattress that swayed and rocked and just seemed to send him sinking into her even deeper. His mouth went to her throat. He licked and kissed.

His cock drove into her. Withdrew. Drove in.

His mouth teased. So close...She pushed her neck harder against him. "Bite me," she urged, voice husky. Words she'd never ever thought to say. But she wanted his bite. She wanted every single thing that he had to give her.

His cock withdrew. Drove in.

His teeth pierced her neck.

Pleasure. So much uncontrolled pleasure. Not a wave or a roll. A detonation that destroyed her. The blast consumed Mercy, and she didn't even have the breath to shout his name.

***

Pleasure. Power. Passion. Xavier's body shuddered as he emptied into Mercy and drank from her at the same time. So heady that he couldn't control himself. Sparks of energy danced in the air around him as his magic slipped its leash. His climax wouldn't stop. Neither would hers.

Too fucking good.

But he had to be careful. He couldn't take too much blood from her. Mercy couldn't be hurt.

He licked her neck. Kissed her skin. Inhaled her scent.

And thrust into her once more.

The only heaven I will ever know.

The thought shouldn't have come to his mind. But it did. And he knew it was true.

Xavier forced his head to lift. He was balls deep in Mercy, and there was no other place in this world—or any of the others—that he'd rather be. He'd never experienced so much pleasure in his life.

And when he looked down at her, the faint shine had her gorgeous body practically glowing for him. But her eyes were closed. Her thick lashes cast shadows over her cheeks.

"Mercy?" Fear slid through him. *How much did I take from you?*

Her lashes fluttered open. She stared up at him. No fear. No worry. Instead, she looked at him with something that seemed to be a whole lot like—

No. No. Xavier shut down the thought.

Then she smiled. "You were worth waiting for."

Automatically, his head shook. No, he wasn't. He was evil. Cursed. He only knew how to destroy and wreck. He wrecked lives. Worlds. He'd brought her there to wreck her. To use her.

To destroy...her.

But she was smiling at him. And saying he was...*worth waiting for*.

She was so wrong.

He opened his mouth to tell her that very thing, to shatter her ill-conceived notions of him, and he said, "So were you."

A truth. A kindness.

He waited for pain to knife through him. Or at least, for the hives to come. Only nothing happened. Nothing but the strange warmth seeping through his chest.

He should withdraw from her. Leave the bed. Put some distance between them. And he did withdraw, though he hated the torture of leaving her tight, hot body. She gave a little cry, and *it* knifed through him the way a good act normally would. "What happened?" He shifted to his side so he could be close to her, but no longer *in* the temptation of her body. "I hurt you, didn't I?"

The light didn't leave her eyes. "Any pain was worth it."

It should not be.

He swallowed and looked away.

Then he heard her yawn. "Stay with me?" she asked sleepily. "I feel better...when you're close."

She should not. She should be repelled. She should have always been repelled by him. Yet, she wasn't. And he wasn't leaving her. Instead, he curled his body around hers. He pulled her close. He put his hand over her stomach, then let it rise until his hand rested over her heart. When he looked down, he could see the shine peeking through his fingers.

The shine he was supposed to take.

When he took her life.

His eyes squeezed closed. Sometimes, he hated being a monster.

CHAPTER EIGHT

"Be careful what you wish for. Especially in a cursed well."

-Life (and Death) Lessons from Xavier Hollow

"You're *sure* that you saw her at this well?" Thomas Durant demanded as he glared at the two waitresses. "You said she ate here with that big, arrogant bastard, you peeked out and saw her making a wish at the well...and then what?" He felt like pulling his damn hair out.

The two waitresses looked at one another. They didn't answer.

Thomas hauled a hundred-dollar bill out of his wallet. "Look, I had a security team watching her." He tried to gentle his tone as he added, "She's under my protection. The now missing woman is my boss's daughter, you see. I promised to look out for her. And the man she's with? He's very bad news." So bad the prick had neutralized Thomas with only a thought.

Xavier Hollow.

Yes, he knew exactly who his enemy was. Defeating the jerk? That was the challenge. But he was better prepared now. He wore a crystal around his neck that would block any of the bastard's compulsions, and he'd picked up a perfect weapon for this fight. And fight he would...once he found Xavier and Mercy. "My team followed her here." His orders. Good thing he'd had them waiting outside of her house. He'd been fucking incapacitated and unable to do jack shit until Xavier's compulsion had worn away. "Only my men swear they never saw her leave this place." He held the money in the air. "Just tell me where she went after making the wish at the well, and I'll give you the cash."

Neither woman reached for the cash. They did back up.

Playing hardball, were they? Fine. He took out another hundred. "Here. One for each of you, if you'll just tell me where my friend went."

Laughter came from a few feet away, mingling with the continuous trickle of water that fell from the nearby fountain. What was up with this place and water? The courtyard had both a massive fountain and the old, kinda creepy well. Plus, twisting vines snaked across the top of the whole outside dining area, pretty much blocking the sunlight and sending shadows snaking in every direction.

But that laughter had his head snapping to the left. Thomas found a man sitting on the edge of the fountain. Blond. Well-dressed. An amused smile played at his lips.

"Leave the women alone. They can't tell you what they don't know. They didn't actually *see* your, ah, friend leave." The man slowly rose. "The shadows were too dark, and even though they were peeking outside—when they clearly should not have been—they couldn't see a thing."

The two women turned and fled.

Thomas was left alone in the courtyard with... "Who the hell are you?"

The man's smile stretched. "I am your new best friend."

"Doubtful. Highly doubtful." Disgusted, Thomas whirled back toward the old well. He grabbed the stone edge and peered down inside. Nothing. Water dripped from some stupid, old bucket and poured down into a dirty pit. Why the hell was he wasting his time?

Because I have to find her. She's worth too much to just let her vanish.

"You have to use a special coin to travel that way."

The blond guy had sidled close. Like, very close. Stiffening, Thomas glanced his way once more. The man was nearly right beside Thomas.

"Hi, there," the stranger practically purred. "Remember me? Your new best friend?"

Who was this creep? "Get the hell away from me."

The man's lips curled down in a pout. "That is no way to talk to your best friend."

"Fuck off." He needed to go check in with the two security men he'd left outside of the restaurant. Maybe they'd seen something else—

A random ray of sunlight hit the object the blond stranger held. The light glinted, became even brighter, and the man began to twirl the object...

A coin.

A shining, silver coin.

"You have to pay the fee in order to travel that way. Luckily for you, I happen to have a spare coin that you can use. I'll give it to you, or, rather, I'll trade it to you. But I do hope you have something I will want in return."

Okay, he was dealing with a psycho. Not his first run-in with the crazies. "Have fun spinning your coin." He whirled away and started marching for the black, wrought-iron gates that would take him out of the courtyard.

"Don't you want to find the descendant?"

Thomas stopped his march. The hair on the nape of his neck rose. He spun around so fast his whole body shook.

The stranger smiled. "I know what she is. So does Xavier. That's why he took her. She's not in your world any longer. She's in his."

That was not good news. "How do I get her back?" He wasn't going to waste time acting like he didn't know what this dick meant. One word—descendant—had convinced Thomas that he wasn't dealing with someone who was crazy or high on drugs. He was just dealing with someone who knew the supernatural score.

Someone like me.

"You use this coin. You toss it into the well. You wish to be taken to her." A shrug. "And you will be."

Thomas bounded toward the other male and tried to snatch the coin from his fingers—

"Nope." The man fisted the coin. "Told you, I'll accept a trade for it." His gaze swept over Thomas. "Now what do you have that I want?"

"You can't barter for the descendant. I'll put her up for auction again when I have her back." No way would he change those plans, but, grudgingly, he allowed, "I'll make sure you're at the auction." The first time, he'd limited attendance. The stupid werewolves had ruined his party. He'd been warned not to include them. That they could get too wild. But they had so much money...

The temptation had been too great.

Then those pricks just tried to steal her!

"I was aware of the last auction. Not invited, of course, but aware. Alas, by the time I arrived, Xavier had already swooped in and stolen your prize."

I am going to kill that bastard. Xavier had ruined everything. Thomas's hands clenched into fists.

"So...just to be clear..." A murmur from the stranger. *"You* are the one trying to sell the descendant. You and her stepfather?"

Thomas laughed. "The old man has no clue." A small sprite rushed toward him from the darkness, and Thomas batted it away with barely a glance.

The blond blinked. "Changeling."

Thomas lifted his chin. "I haven't been called that in a while."

"You saw the sprite. Clear as day for you. Humans might catch glimpses when they are in enchanted places like this courtyard, but you just had more than a glimpse. Way more. You punched the poor bastard right in his face."

Yes, he had. "Can't stand sprites. No one steals from me."

"I'll remember that." Once more, the stranger's gaze swept over him. "You look like a human. Smell like a human. But you see the sprites. You're a definite changeling. Did you always know?"

"Know that someone killed the real baby that my so-called parents had and left me in his place?" Because that was the way humans always wound up with a changeling child. The human baby was taken. Typically killed. A fairy infant was put in the human child's place. Left there to cause havoc.

Or hell.

Thomas loved both things. "My real father visited me frequently. I always knew the score."

"How wonderful for you." His new "friend" craned to look around Thomas's back. "Don't see wings."

"My father cut them off me so the humans wouldn't know what I really was."

A blink. "What a sweetheart of a father you have. I've got one of those, too."

Like he gave a shit about this jerk's father. "I don't need wings."

"But you do need a descendant."

Did this jackass get how valuable Mercy was? "I can get an army in exchange for her! A lifetime of spells from warlocks! Vampires will give me immortality. I can have *everything*." He'd known it the minute he saw her.

Eighteen years old. Shuddering and terrified because her mother had just died right in front of her.

I did that, too. I found the mother and sold her first.

But he'd needed to wait a bit before putting Mercy up for sale. She'd needed to really come into her shine. The brighter the shine, the more valuable the descendant. So he'd gotten close to her stepfather. He'd fed Mercy the pills so that she'd stop seeing monsters and so that no other paranormals would know what she was. He'd waited until she'd aged and he knew she'd be at her peak.

Then I started putting sugar pills in the bottle. Mixing them with the real deal so that her shine could slip through. And the real deal? That had been a bit of fairy dust. Courtesy of his father. His father had brought him the most powerful magic to keep Mercy's shine hidden from others. *And my father expects to make quite the bounty when we sell her.*

And if he didn't get the bounty...Thomas swallowed. Disappointing his father wasn't an option. "I need a descendant," Thomas snapped. "Tell me what you want."

"Easy. I want your soul."

Thomas laughed.

The stranger didn't.

Thomas leaned forward, as if the joke was truly hilarious. His hand reached inside of his coat. And, in a flash, he whipped out the knife he'd brought along. A knife made of iron and infused with fey magic. *Didn't have this with me when I first crossed paths with Xavier.* He'd just been packing silver bullets because he expected werewolves to be the worst enemies he faced at the ball. This time, though, he'd come ready for someone with Xavier's power.

The fey knew that iron was extremely effective against a dark enemy.

He lunged forward and drove the knife into his so-called new best friend's stomach. He withdrew it, then stabbed the bastard over and over again. A gasping cry came from the man even as blood began to trickle past his lips.

It was over quickly. It always was. Thomas snagged a napkin from a nearby table and wiped the blood off his knife. Then he put the weapon back in its sheath. Blood covered the fool who'd tried to barter with him.

"My soul isn't for sale," Thomas told him. He leaned over the fallen man and took the coin from his lifeless hand. "But thanks for the shiny coin, asshole." Whistling, he rolled back his shoulders and turned for the well. "I wish to be where Mercy is." He dropped the coin.

Nothing happened.

Sonofabitch.

He glared and peered down into the well. This was some bullshit. This was—

Something was moving in the bottom of the well. Swirling. He could feel wind against his face. Wind that came from within the well.

Thomas nodded. Now he got it. The well was a corridor. His father used magic corridors all the time.

But this would be Thomas's first trip through one.

How bad could it be?

He hopped over the wall of the well and vanished.

***

He waited until the fool jumped into the well. Then Paxton waved his hand and let the illusion disappear. He wasn't the one on the ground.

Blood covered a long, black snake.

Paxton left his spot near the fountain and rushed toward the well. And he just could not hold back his laughter. "You dumb sonofabitch." *That* was how you got a soul. So easy. "You took the coin to get passage to Mercy." His hand shoved into his pocket, and he brought out a second coin. "But how the hell do you expect to get back?"

Without another coin, there would be no return trip.

Paxton laughed even harder.

Then, from the corner of his eye, he saw the smoke drifting from the dead snake's body. His laughter stilled. His head whipped around.

A normal knife wouldn't have burned his creation that way. A normal knife...

Oh, hell. The changeling hadn't been using a normal knife. He'd been using something much, much more powerful.

Fuck me. Paxton immediately dropped the coin into the well. *I wish to see my brother. I wish to see my brother.* But the well didn't change. The corridor didn't open.

Even with the coin, he was still locked out. His wish wasn't working.

And the only brother he even *somewhat* liked—despite the appearance he gave because Paxton was, after all, the king of illusions—his brother had no idea a changeling assassin was coming for him.

Paxton had to get the well to open for him. Even if he had to break the bitch down stone by stone...

CHAPTER NINE

*"Hold tight to the things that matter. Kill any
fools who try to take what's yours.
Oh, that's uncivilized? Like I give a shit."*

-*Life (and Death) Lessons from Xavier Hollow*

"Your evilness?"

"G'away."

A throat cleared. "Your most wretched evilness?"

"Sleeping."

"Your most dastardly, wretched evilness?" A touch of impatience. Then... *"Ahem."*

Something *poked* Xavier in the upper arm. Something annoying. His eyes flew open, and he found himself looking up at Micah's worried face.

Micah...who was leaning over the bed.

The bed I'm sharing with Mercy. A naked Mercy. Xavier lifted the hand that wasn't currently looped around Mercy. Flames danced over his fingers as he told Micah, "If she's naked and you're looking at her, I will burn the hair from your head."

Micah swallowed. "You...know she's not my type, right?"

Like that mattered to him. *"Burn the hair from—"*

"She has a sheet over her, my king! I can't see a thing!" Micah's eyes closed. "Though *your* dick is waving around, and what a great wave it is doing."

A growl burst from Xavier. He summoned some quick power and made sure to put a silken gown over Mercy before he donned his usual black attire. He did not, however, get out of the bed. He was comfortable where he was. "You can open your eyes, but keep your voice *quiet.*" They'd both been whispering so far.

He didn't want to wake up Mercy.

Even as he had the thought, Xavier braced for pain. Only...

None came.

Odd as hell. In the past, every good act had led to instant pain for him. But now, it seemed as if the pain were more...intermittent. Random.

Fleeting.

"You need to come with me," Micah murmured. "We have to talk, privately."

He'd figured Micah would say something like that. "I'm happy here."

"You're...what?"

Xavier's head turned so he could stare over at Mercy. In sleep, she was freaking adorable. "I'm going to keep her." There. Done. Decision made. "Now, let me get back to sleep." The best sleep he'd had in...forever. His eyes closed.

"Your diabolical evilness..."

Xavier sighed.

"Your twisted corruptness..."

He opened his eyes.

"We must talk," Micah rasped. "At once. It's about the pills...They *did* stop her from seeing monsters and they dulled her shine..."

In a blink, Xavier was out of the bed. On his feet. Towering over his advisor. But, no, they couldn't *talk* there. Mercy was sleeping. Xavier marched for the door and swung it open. Micah scurried out with him.

With one last look at his sleeping Mercy, Xavier closed the door. He crossed his arms over his chest—the better to stop himself from throwing fire if this was news he didn't like—and he glared at Micah. "Tell me. Everything."

But Micah was busy looking at the closed door. "You got her to give up her world and come to yours."

Xavier grunted. Yes, so?

"You...you took her virginity."

"More like she *gave* it to me," he corrected, oddly annoyed. "Not like I stole it. She kissed me first. Then she let me taste all of her..." Her taste—so insanely good.

Micah's wide eyes rolled toward Xavier.

"Then the pleasure took us." Xavier shrugged.

"She gave up her world. Her body. The only thing left...is her life." Micah sent Xavier an encouraging smile. "You almost have her."

Xavier's spine straightened. "There is no *almost* in this equation. I do have her. She's mine." Hadn't Micah heard him before? Odd, usually his advisor's sense of hearing was perfect. "I'm keeping her."

Micah backed up a step. "You...can't."

"I can."

Micah shook his head. "You *can't.*"

Xavier's hands dropped to his sides. Fire began to spin.

"You know that you can't!" Micah backed up another step. "If she doesn't give up her life for you, then you will lose your power. Is that how you want to live? Weak? *I* live that way. I would have died that way. You do not want that life."

Xavier glared at him. *I do not want her death.*

"You won't be able to protect Mercy with no power. She shines so brightly. Without your power, you will lose control here. Others will come after her. They will rip her apart right in front of you."

The balls of flames at Xavier's sides spun faster.

"Then in the end, you will be destroyed, too. There is no choice. She has to break your curse." Sympathy flashed on Micah's face. "I'm sorry."

Xavier lifted his right hand. The flames rose with the movement. "You dare to pity me? Me, the king of destruction, the breaker of spirits, the eradicator of hope—"

"I do feel badly for you, my king," Micah told him quietly. "Because *you* just realized what it is like to love. And now you are going to have to kill the one thing you love in all of the many worlds that exist. Your father's curse was truly more wicked than I realized."

No. "I do not love." Not Mercy. Not anyone. Love was a weakness. A human emotion that had somehow infected far too many monsters. But it had not—and *would* not ever—infect Xavier. "I had great sex with her. She amuses me. Nothing more."

Micah watched him. "You've never wanted to keep someone before."

"I let you stay, didn't I?" His gaze strayed to the shut door. Mercy slept beyond that door. *I do not love her.*

"I wouldn't leave." A pause. "I had nowhere to go. You *did* massacre half my pack, if you recall."

"Oh, was that me?"

"You did it when you found me in the woods. Surrounded by those bastards. They'd already nearly sliced me to ribbons. I was in so much pain I could barely move. And I was only ten years old." He sniffed.

"Don't you dare cry on me," Xavier warned. His gaze shot back to Micah.

Sure enough, Micah was sniffling even harder.

"Dammit, *stop.*" Xavier's flames died away.

"You jumped in front of me. You took the slices from their claws. Your blood rained down on me. You told them to stop. Told them to retreat or die. They laughed. Said they were not stopping until I was in pieces." Emotion broke in every word.

Xavier winced. Micah *knew* he had a rule in place about this shit. "There is no point in getting yourself worked up like this," Xavier snapped. "They are not worth it."

"You burned them when they tried to take me. Not the little fire you send at me. You incinerated them into ash in an instant."

The same way he'd incinerated the werewolves at Mercy's home. *You do not hurt those under my protection.*

"Why did you save me that day?" Micah asked him as he blinked his watery eyes.

"I was bored."

Micah shook his head.

"Fine. I was...in the mood to kill some werewolves."

Again, Micah shook his head.

This was getting annoying. "I didn't like the unfairness of the fight. Two against ten were far better odds than one against ten."

Still, Micah shook his head.

"You tell me!" Xavier burst out. "Why did I save you? Why did I—"

"Even as you saved me, pain nearly sent you to the ground. I could see the agony on your face. I didn't understand why back then." Micah hauled a shaking hand through his thin hair. "It was because you were doing something good."

Xavier's chin notched up. "How dare you."

"You aren't supposed to do good things. But sometimes, you slip up." Micah's voice lowered even more. "Even though it hurts you, even though your father made it so that you were *never* supposed to be good, sometimes, you still do things that go against your nature. Things like...save a runt werewolf who will always be weak."

"You're the slyest, smartest bastard I know. So what if you can't shift? You've helped me outwit our enemies plenty of times."

Micah blushed. "Thank you, I-I do like to think I'm clever."

He was. A clever and manipulative bastard.

"But, my king, the truth is that you saved a runt. You saved me...and now you want to save *her*."

I will not kill her. "There will be another way to break the curse."

"You want to save her because you look at her, and you see something really, truly good. Not just the shine. *Her*. And you don't want to break that goodness."

I don't want to break her.

"But, my wicked one, if you don't take her life, you will lose yours. Then...what do you think will happen to her? Mercy has a shine. She will always be a target. The pills camouflaged her shine for a time, but she is no longer taking them. She *shouldn't* keep taking them. I think they are linked to old, fey power. It is the strangest thing. Half of the pills in the bottle are pure sugar, but the others? The ones I suspect she actually took for years? They contained fairy dust."

Rage flashed in Xavier's eyes.

Micah kept talking, quickly. "As long as she shines, others will come for her. They will not stop until she is ripped apart. Don't you see?" Micah swallowed with a rough click of sound. "You will do her a kindness if you make her death quick."

Xavier heard the rush of footsteps beyond the closed bedroom door. Mercy was awake and hurrying toward them. Tensing, he schooled his expression. Since when had it become so hard to do that? The door swung open, and his Mercy stood there. A wide smile curled her lips, and her amber eyes were lit with wonder.

"Xavier!"

Mercy said his name with joy. *Joy.* No one else had ever done that.

Then she threw her body against his and hugged him. "There are dragons flying outside of the window!"

Yes, there were. Ferocious beasts bigger than the buses in her human world. With more teeth than any great white shark could dream of having. And with enough fire power to decimate a town.

"They are *beautiful!*" She eased back and beamed at him. "Absolutely the most gorgeous creatures I have ever seen!"

They were monsters. Bringers of death. And she thought they were gorgeous?

Mercy glanced toward an avid Micah, flushed a rosy red, then leaned close to Xavier once more and whispered, "I missed you when I woke up."

She'd missed him?

Xavier nodded. Decision made. He spared his advisor a brief glance and announced, "I'm keeping her." And if anyone tried to take her, he and his army of dragons would *decimate* them. "You think *they* are gorgeous?" he asked her.

"Yes." Awe filled the word.

"Then wait until you see *me* fly." He flashed magic her way because she couldn't just head out in the gown. Not if she was flying. He gave her jeans and a comfy shirt. Cute little black boots. Then he twined his fingers with hers. "Let's go."

No hesitation. She came with him eagerly.

Until Micah stepped into their path. "What are you *doing?*" Alarm hitched in his voice. "There's not a lot of time left!"

"Screw the curse," Xavier said.

"No." Micah shook his head, frantic. "No. No, *you can't!*"

"I'm the king of destruction. I can do any damn thing I want. And right now..." He lifted Mercy's hand to his mouth and kissed her knuckles. "I'm going to fly."

***

No, no, no, no, no. In horror, Micah watched as Xavier strolled away. His king was holding hands with the descendant. Acting as if he didn't have a care in the world.

When he should have every care. When he should be frantically worried that he would lose his power.

What is happening?

Something was wrong with his king. Something was putting him in mortal jeopardy. And that something...

I think it's her.

He needed to do more research. Not much was known about descendants, but Xavier had a four-story library that housed tome after tome of lore. There *had* to be a section in Xavier's library about descendants. And any abilities they had to control others... He just had to hurry. Had to find the right intel. Had to help his king.

Because if Xavier died...

I'll be next. Micah was only alive because of Xavier. Without him...*someone will finally come to collect on my father's old offer.*

Someone would come to take Micah's head.

His hand rose to his neck. He could survive without many things. Because of the magic that Xavier had gifted him years ago, Micah could heal from most injuries. He could even—and had—regrown his arms. Not that Xavier had taken his arms, despite what the king liked to boast. That had been an unfortunate dragon attack. Micah probably shouldn't have tried to ride the beasts. Everyone knew you couldn't ride untamed dragons.

Xavier had given him the magic as Micah screamed in agony. His limbs had slowly come back.

One of the benefits of Xavier's magics? Micah could now heal from any fire. But...

But he couldn't survive losing his head. Very few paranormals could.

So he would *not* be losing it. No matter what he had to do.

CHAPTER TEN

"Know what's real torture? Having hope. Then losing it."

-Life (and Death) Lessons from Xavier Hollow

The dragons were massive. Their scales gleamed beneath the sunlight. A sunlight that seemed even brighter than what she'd had, um, well, in the human realm.

Mercy wasn't exactly sure *where* this realm was or even what it was, but the place was different. Brighter sun. Clouds that were a faint purple. Trees that sprang far too high in the sky. And, of course, the dragons.

There definitely hadn't been flying dragons back in New Orleans.

She took a step toward them.

"Nope." Xavier hauled her back. "First rule. No one can ride an untamed dragon. And these beasts..." He inclined his head toward the dragons that had taken to the sky. "All untamed. Well, mostly untamed. They won't harm me. But if anyone else goes too close to them, they get bitey and fire crazy." He winced. "Just ask Micah."

Mercy gulped. "I will definitely not be asking them for a ride." She cut him a glance. "I think you're the only one I ever want biting me."

He smiled at her. No sign of his fangs. Just a real smile. One that had her breath catching because the man was... "You're even more gorgeous than they are."

His smile slipped.

"I was wrong before. *You're* the most gorgeous thing I've ever seen," she blurted and immediately felt awkward. Did great sex do that? Make you extremely awkward? Make you overshare? And speaking of the great sex... "Thank you. For yesterday." She'd slept so soundly in his arms. But she wasn't thanking him for the sleep. "That was more pleasure than I ever dreamed existed."

His smile had vanished completely. The darkness of his eyes shifted to red. He stared at her as if he—

Could eat me alive.

Was someone feeling bitey? "Was it good for you, too?" Mercy whispered.

He flinched.

Uh, oh. "I used the 'g' word." Mercy shook her head. "I am so sorry! Let me try again." She cleared her throat. "Was it just as terrible, awful, and wretched for you? So wretched that you want to do it again and again and again?"

He hauled her close. His mouth crashed down onto hers. The kiss was everything she wanted. Passion and need. A hunger so consuming it surged through her whole body. Possession. Craving.

Her fingers curled over his powerful shoulders. Her mouth opened wider. Yes, yes, yes! She loved his kiss. Loved the way he could make desire careen wildly past all her control. She loved...him.

Mercy jerked back. Her eyes flew open, and she stared at him in shock.

"Again and again and again," he assured her in a voice that was little more than a growl. "Like I told Micah, I want to keep you."

Mercy shook her head. "You don't keep people."

He shrugged. "You're safe here. I won't let any monsters hunt you." He looked toward the dragons. "If any of your enemies should slip to my land, I'll let the dragons eat them. Won't that be fun?"

Fun wasn't the right word. "I..." Mercy stopped.

His shoulders stiffened. "You don't want to stay with me."

"Actually, I think staying with you would be incredible."

His stare flew back to her. Shock filled his red gaze.

"But I need to let my stepfather know I'm okay." Something that had been nagging at her. "Maybe I can call him?"

"We don't have service here, sweetheart."

Right. "Can I send him a note? Write a letter? I just don't want him to worry about me."

Now his red eyes narrowed. "You get that he could be your enemy, don't you? Someone close wanted you to think that you were crazy. Someone had you on some kind of magic pills so that you'd stop seeing monsters and so that your shine would be hidden. Someone knew exactly what you were all these years."

"He's the only family I have." A painful truth. "I don't want him to be the enemy." Her vision went a little blurry with tears.

"Don't," he ordered. "Don't you dare cry."

She looked upward in an attempt to stop the tears from falling.

"Fuck." Angry. Then..."What would make you happy right now? Tell me. I'll give it to you. What will make you stop crying?"

"I—"

"Got it." He snapped his fingers together and vanished.

But she hadn't told him anything!

He reappeared about twenty feet away. "You like dragons." His powerful voice carried easily to her. "Then I'll give you a dragon you can ride." His hands flew into the air, and then he began to change. To grow bigger. So much bigger. Dark black scales exploded over his body as he seemed to burst into the twisting, churning shape of...a dragon.

Shock held her immobile.

A long, spiked tail extended from his body and slammed into the ground. Two big, flapping wings sprang from his back and sent wind hurtling toward her body.

She couldn't remain immobile any longer. The wind had her stumbling back. But before she could fall, he was there. The dragon swooped toward her, and one wickedly long claw caught her. He tossed her onto his back as if it was the most normal thing in the world.

Hold on. Xavier's voice. But she only heard the order in her head.

She didn't know what she was supposed to hold. Her hands flew down and curved under the pointed edge of a ginormous scale. Then, they were off. He lunged straight up into the sky and all she could do was hold on for dear life...and scream her head off.

***

The scream caught him off guard. One moment, Thomas was wandering around lost in some godforsaken forest. *Take me to Mercy, my ass.* He'd been dropped in the middle of nowhere. He'd been swearing and cursing a blue streak for fucking hours.

The only *good* thing that had happened to him? Right after he'd landed, another silver coin had come hurtling after him. The thing had slammed into his head, and he'd grabbed it before it could drop to the ground.

My ticket back home. He didn't know how or why the coin had come to hurtle at him, but he'd just been grateful. *Changeling luck.* He'd always had it.

Only that luck had seemed to fail because he couldn't find Mercy. His feet ached, hunger gnawed at him, sweat soaked him and—

Then he heard a woman's scream.

A scream...of delight.

A cry that came from overhead.

He looked up, and his jaw nearly hit the ground. A giant, black dragon streaked across the too bright sky like some kind of enveloping shadow. And riding on that dragon's back? *Mercy.* She was screaming with joy and laughing and holding tightly to the dragon.

She was also flying away.

"No!" Thomas bellowed. "Mercy, come back here!" He raced after her, trying his best to keep up with her and her racing dragon. Only that was an impossible task. Because who the hell could keep up with an actual dragon? His breath heaved in and out. In and out.

They couldn't fly forever. They had to come down sooner or later and when they did—

I will get you.

Except...

He could hear growls from behind him. A lot of growls.

He staggered to a stop. Thomas whipped out his knife and spun to face the threat.

Four black panthers prowled out of the forest. Sleek but muscled. His sweaty fingers gripped the knife. "You're not...normal panthers, are you?"

He could have sworn the panther in the front smiled at him. Then it opened its mouth to reveal what looked like several hundred razor-sharp teeth.

"Fuck!" Thomas yelled.

The panthers attacked, and he slashed out with his knife.

***

The dragon landed but Mercy's heart stayed in her throat. The ride through the sky had been the most exhilarating, the most thrilling, the most amazing thing—

The dragon shifted in a flash of light. Scales vanished. His massive size disappeared. And she barely had time to gasp before she found herself riding...

A naked Xavier. He was on the ground. She straddled him.

He rolled quickly, and she was suddenly beneath him on the soft grass. He rose above her. A smile lifted his lips and lit his eyes. "Have fun?"

"That was incredible."

"You weren't scared?"

Her hand rose and touched his cheek. "How could I have been? I was with you."

His lashes flickered. For a moment, he almost looked sad. That scared her. Xavier had never looked that way. "What's wrong?"

"I am."

Clothes appeared on his body.

Unnecessary. She'd hoped to tempt him to another delicious round of lovemaking—

"I am wrong, Mercy."

She shook her head. "Don't say that."

"I'm the monster—"

"You are mine!" Did she sound possessive? Too bad. She was. If he got to say that he was keeping her, then she got to say that he was hers. "To me, you're perfect. You saved me. Over and over again. You are not bad, Xavier. You are good." He'd just taken her on a ride through the clouds. He'd given her an experience better than a dream. He—

"I tricked you."

Mercy felt a shiver rake over her.

"I needed you to give up your life for me. And you did. So easily. You came with me, and you barely hesitated."

The shiver turned into a colder chill. "What are you talking about?"

He rose and pulled Mercy to her feet. Then his hand went over her chest. Over her heart. "Monsters want to take your shine."

She couldn't speak.

"The others want to rip you apart to get it. But I was just going to get you to surrender it to me. I was going to get you to give up your life for me."

She wanted to slam her hands over her ears so that she couldn't hear his words. But that was what a child did, right? When you tried to stop something you didn't want to hear?

Her gaze darted upward. The bright sun seemed to have dimmed. The purple clouds were even darker. The place didn't look so beautiful and warm any longer.

More stark. Foreboding.

Evil?

"I had three days to win you. Three days to take your life."

"No." That was all she could manage. Just... "No." No, he wasn't saying these things. Xavier had helped her. Had saved her. He wasn't standing there telling her that he'd...planned to kill her? A tear slid down her cheek.

I made love with him.

I-I...love him?

He'd tricked her into loving him?

Or had she just fallen into that trap all by herself?

"You saved me." Mercy was adamant. She would not doubt him. She couldn't. Her whole life, she'd never felt this way about anyone. There was just an utter certainty inside herself that he was *right*. That he was hers. "At the ball, you protected me—"

"I stole you for myself."

"You took a bullet—"

"And it allowed me to take your blood. Your power. See, that's what I have to do. I'm not savage like the other beasts. I can take your shine one sweet drop of power at a time." His hands balled into fists. "That's what I've been doing. By the time I was finished, you would have offered your throat and begged me to take everything."

She rocked back as if he'd hit her. "No." His bite had brought her pleasure. Not pain. Not...death.

"Yes."

Instead of rocking back again, she surged toward him. Mercy's hands locked around his arms. *"No!* I won't believe it! You weren't just going to kill me!"

His eyes burned so red.

"You care about me!" she blasted at him. "You saved me. You protected me. You just flew me through the sky to make me laugh. You *care.*" Mercy's chin lifted as her hold tightened on him. "I have faith in you."

"You should not." Grim.

"You are not going to kill me!" Mercy screamed at him.

He shook his head. "No, I'm not."

Right. She knew this. "Then why the hell would you ever say—"

"Because that was the original plan. Until I realized that I'd rather have no power than live in a world without you."

What? Her eyes widened. "Xavier?"

"When I said I want to keep you..." He swallowed. "I think...I think humans would have instead said...I-I love you." A stumble, a stutter, when Xavier didn't stumble or stutter. "I...believe that's what I feel. I can't say for certain. I've never felt this way before."

"What way?" Her head was spinning. He'd just said he'd sought her out to steal her shine. *Like the other monsters.* Only now he was saying that he loved her? "What way do you feel?"

"Like I would give my life for you. Like I would do anything to protect you and the shine you carry. Like you matter more than anything else." His jaw locked. "Like I want to be *good* for you, even though that is something I will never, ever be."

She couldn't speak.

"That's why I'm telling you how we began. So you will know my secrets. I tricked you when we met. I was never the hero. But you make me want to be so much more than the beast."

"Xavier, I—"

"I can't be more." Rasped. "I don't know how. But...*I want to keep you.*"

Those words...she understood now. For him, keeping someone with him, that was love. Protecting them. Shielding them. Her body slammed against his as she hugged him fiercely. "You are more. You are everything."

"You can't...you can't still want to touch me, not after what I told you. After what I-I planned...you can't..."

She eased back and stared up at him. "You could never do it."

"What?"

"You could never hurt me."

"Mercy..."

"Because you don't hurt what you love."

"Sometimes, you do." So rough and broken. "I've seen it happen. I never, ever want to hurt you. I have to find a way to protect your shine. I have to find a way to keep you alive."

Her lips parted to reply.

But then she heard the snarls. The growls.

In a flash, Xavier grabbed her and whipped her behind him. He used his body as a shield to protect her from the threat charging at them. She peeked around his side, trying to see the danger they faced.

Panthers? Muscled, powerful, with sleek, black fur and...dragging something.

Dragging...a body.

They dropped the body at Xavier's feet. Snarled once more before whirling. Without ever glancing back, the panthers bounded away.

"How the fuck did he get here?" Xavier demanded.

Mercy hauled her gaze off the fleeing panthers and looked at the body. It took her a moment to see past the thick blood and all the savage wounds to realize that she was staring at a familiar figure. "Thomas!" She tried to lunge for him.

Xavier pushed her back. "Stay away from him."

"But, Xavier, I think he's still alive!" She'd glimpsed his chest moving. Hadn't she? At first, she'd thought for sure the panthers were bringing a dead body to Xavier. Kind of the way a house cat would drop a snake at your feet to proudly show off his kill.

But...

Thomas may still be alive.

"He shouldn't be here." Anger and confusion roughened Xavier's voice. "He shouldn't be in my realm. How the fuck did he get here?"

Her gaze fell to Thomas once more. Horror and nausea had her stomach twisting. *So much brutality.* The panthers had sliced him with their claws and bitten him with their teeth. Wounds covered him. But he was still breathing. Faintly. He let out a pain-filled moan.

Mercy broke from Xavier and rushed for Thomas.

"No!" Xavier grabbed her around the waist. "Fucking shine. It always makes you want to *help* and—"

Thomas's eyes opened. Pain filled his gaze, yes, but so did determination. And she realized that he'd been waiting for this moment. Seeming to be weaker than he was. Her lips parted in shock because he'd lunged up in an instant, and he'd brought out a knife that had been hidden beneath his bloody clothes and he was driving that knife right toward her.

Xavier spun with her in his arms. The knife missed her. But it hit him. It plunged into his back.

She was staring right at Xavier when the blade drove into him. She saw his eyes widen with startled surprise. Saw the red of his gaze—the red instantly faded to black. And a plume of smoke rose from his back.

"Mercy..." Xavier breathed her name.

And then he pushed her away from him.

Mercy nearly lost her footing, and she staggered in an attempt to stay upright. With horror, she watched Thomas hacking at Xavier's back with the knife. Over and over again. "No!" Mercy screamed.

Xavier sagged to his knees. His face was a mask of agony, and in that desperate moment, she didn't know if the pain came from the knife wounds—wounds that were sending smoke rushing into the air behind him—or because Xavier had just done something good. He'd risked himself to save her.

And hadn't he told her before...if he did a good enough act...

Can't it kill him?

"No!" Another cry from her, but this one shook with fury. She didn't retreat. She launched herself at Thomas. Flew right at him and ignored the slash of the knife as it slid over her shoulder. The pain didn't matter. What mattered was stopping that knife from plunging into Xavier again.

She and Thomas hit the ground. But, frenzied, he kept slashing. She brought up her hand, and the knife cut across her wrist. "Stop!" Her other forearm came up defensively.

"Mercy?" The knife froze. "What the hell am I doing? I need you alive!" He dropped the knife and grabbed her. He stumbled to his feet and locked one arm around her stomach as he dragged her with him. "You aren't worth anything dead. Had to play fucking possum with those damn panthers...knew they'd bring me to their master..."

Xavier sprawled on the ground. He'd landed on his back. Smoke drifted around him.

"Not so unstoppable now, is he? And he's not the one with the power. He can't control me with a compulsion, not while I wear my charm, but I can sure hurt *him*." Thomas laughed, but the sound was weak because his blood loss was very real. She could feel the warm wetness of his blood against her. "I used an enchanted blade from my father. Made of iron and fairy dust. Can weaken even the monster kings."

Weaken didn't mean kill.

And she'd just seen Xavier's eyes open.

"Time to leave." Thomas opened his left hand, and she glimpsed a silver coin in his palm. "I wish we were back at—"

She elbowed him as hard as she could. And Mercy swiped that coin. She shoved it into her pocket and tore from his hold as she tried to reach for the fallen knife.

"Down," Xavier bellowed.

She got down. Mercy hit the ground.

Flames burst from Xavier's hands. A whirling ball of flames that went straight over her.

"Ah!" A cry of agony.

Mercy knew she shouldn't, but she looked back. Just in time to see flames engulf Thomas's body. They rushed and rolled over him and then he was simply ash.

Her breath heaved out. *Do not be sick. Do not.*

Her wrist throbbed and ached. So did her shoulder. She ignored the blood and hauled herself to Xavier. His hands had fallen back to the earth, and he wasn't trying to get up.

"Xavier?"

His head turned toward her. He smiled. "I...did it."

She grabbed his hand. Why did it feel so cold? He'd just shot flames. Shouldn't his hand feel warm? "You did," she agreed. "You killed him. Thomas won't ever hurt me again."

"You...are beautiful."

Her desperate gaze swept over him. "There's smoke coming from your body. Th-the knife made you weak. You're going to be okay, though?" He had to be okay.

"I...did it," he said again. His voice was even softer. Even weaker.

She didn't like for her Xavier to be weak. "Yes, you killed—"

"Did...something good. For you." His eyes closed.

No, no, no. "Xavier!"

His eyes didn't open. He didn't seem to be breathing. He had to breathe, right? In order to live? There was so much he hadn't gone over about this whole paranormal world, but she distinctly remembered him saying...*Monsters eat. We dream. We fuck.*

They had to breathe, too. Only Xavier didn't seem to be breathing. And—

She shoved her bloody wrist over his mouth. No hesitation. No regret. "You take my blood. You take my shine. It made you better before. It will make you better now."

He wasn't drinking.

She pried open his lips. Squeezed her wrist and made more blood come out. "You *take* it!"

Still nothing. "No!" Mercy was screaming and crying, and Xavier was dying before her. She knew it. The knife wounds might not be what was actually killing him. *She* could be the one causing his agony...because Mercy had gotten him to do an act too good.

He sacrificed himself for me.

As she watched, the skin of his body began to change. It darkened, and then...pieces broke away. Like ash drifting in the wind.

If the act is big enough, it will be like having all the skin ripped from my body. He'd told her that, and she hadn't fully understood, not until now.

"What have you done?" A frantic cry that came from the right.

Her head snapped toward that cry.

Micah gaped at the sight of Xavier, and tears began to fall down his cheeks.

"You killed my king!"

"No!" She tried to force more blood from her wrist into his mouth, but the blood just fell down his chin and slid over his jaw. "He's not dying! He's not! I'm giving him my shine, and he's going to heal, just like he healed before."

But Xavier wasn't moving.

"Don't you dare do this!" Mercy screamed at him. "Don't you die! *I'm giving you my shine! I'm giving everything to you because I love you! Don't you leave me! Don't!*" She couldn't stop her own tears.

She couldn't do anything but scream and rage and try to force her blood into him. Blood was power. If he got enough power, he'd heal. He'd come back to her.

She'd keep him.

Weakness whispered through her, and her body swayed.

She'd...keep him.

Her head started to sag forward.

Xavier's eyes flew open. Fiery red eyes. His hand flew up and clamped around her wrist, and he began to gorge on her blood.

CHAPTER ELEVEN

"A happy ending? What the fuck is that? Sounds miserable. And boring. How about we go for a bloody, violent ending and enjoy the hell out of the destruction?"

-Life (and Death) Lessons from Xavier Hollow

Mercy fell beside him, and Xavier instantly snapped to his senses. A bellow of fear and fury burst from him as he lunged for her.

"My king!" Micah's startled cry.

Xavier felt power pour through his body. Power and warmth and strength and he was terrified. Shaking so badly as he tried to pick up Mercy and run with her back to his castle.

There was magic in the castle. If he got her there, she'd be okay. She had to be all right.

I took too much. I don't see her shine. There was no soft glow from his Mercy. Just shadows. His shadows as they tried to envelop her.

"Help me!" Xavier thundered back at Micah. Micah was smart. So clever. He could usually figure out anything.

And Xavier was running too fucking slowly. He let wings burst from his back. The wings of the dragon that he'd been earlier. Mercy had laughed as she rode him, and he'd loved her joy. He'd just wanted to keep making her laugh. Pain had cut through him at first when he'd taken flight because he'd been doing something freaking *good,* for her, but he hadn't minded the pain because she'd been so happy.

He'd decided that he could live with pain, as long as he had her.

But then the pain had vanished. The flight had brought him as much joy as it had her.

And he'd told her everything. Even told her the worst truth…

I love you.

Now she was still. Her blood was everywhere, and he was terrified. His wings flapped as he raced through the air. Flying was so much faster than running. He flew them back to their bedroom. The room in the castle where she'd given herself to him and where he'd given himself to her.

He crashed through the window and sent glass flying. Mercy didn't stir. If anything, she'd just gone paler.

With shaking hands, he put her on the bed. His wings were still extended, and they scraped against the ceiling.

"Mercy…*please*…"

There was no shine to her. She'd given it to him. To save him. His blood-stained hands flew over her. He'd built this castle. Every single part of it was made of his magic, and he pulled that magic to him as he tried to heal her.

He'd healed Micah. Put him back together. He could do the same for Mercy.

His fingers curled around her still bleeding wrist. Xavier tried to use his power to fix her. Only it didn't work. His hand burned where he touched her, but she didn't heal. Her blood kept pouring through his fingers.

"Micah!" Xavier bellowed. "Micah, *help me!*"

He heard footsteps thundering up the stairs. He'd banished everyone from his castle when he arrived with Mercy. An instant surge of power as soon as she'd crossed into his world because he hadn't wanted anyone else near her. He'd only trusted Micah around her shine.

But in trying to protect her, he'd sent away the creatures who might have been able to assist him with spells to bring her back. Now, she was slipping away.

I have to keep her.

"My king!" Micah burst into the room. He ran to the bed, and his eyes nearly bulged from his head. "Her shine is gone." His gaze rose to Xavier. "You...you have it. I see it. You *glow.*"

Not for long. His body would take her shine and transform it into dark power. The beast that he was fed on dark power.

"She did it!" Micah smiled. "She sacrificed her life for you. The curse is over. You will never be weak. Only strong. No one will ever be able to break you!"

Yes, yes, that was the key. *Clever Micah.* Xavier's advisor was right. He *was* strong.

Powerful. More so than he'd ever been in his life. Xavier brought his wrist to his mouth and bit.

"Uh, my king? Your wickedness?"

Xavier put his wrist to Mercy's mouth. "Drink."

She didn't.

"Ah, your dastardly eminence, what are you doing?"

His cheeks felt wet. "I need her."

"She broke the curse."

Gently, he pushed his wrist against her mouth again. "I will be broken without her." Why wasn't she drinking? She seemed so pale. *Getting paler with each moment that passes.*

"You..." Micah stopped. He scuttled closer to Xavier and grabbed his arm. Micah tried to haul Xavier's arm—and Xavier—away from Mercy. "You're trying to save her?"

"I will keep her." But he meant...*fuck me, I love her. I love her. I love her.* Desperate, he pulled his gaze from Mercy and looked at his friend. "Micah, how can I save her?"

Micah shook his head and stopped trying to haul him away. "You can't, my king. All you do is destroy. You don't save."

"I want to save her." It was the only thing he wanted. "She gave me her blood. It saved me. Blood is power. If she takes my blood, she'll get stronger. Help me get her to take my blood. Micah, *help me!"*

"She's human, and she's dying." Micah backed up a step as he delivered this grim announcement. "You can't save a human. That's not how things work. Not even for you." His expression turned sly. "You're not *really* a vampire. Your bite and your blood won't change her."

"I am the fucking ruler of vampires. And demons. And shifters. I have all their power. I have more power than any of them!" A roar.

"Really?" A careful taunt. "Then prove it. Show me what you really look like. Show me who you are beneath the skin. *Show me your real self.* The self you hide. And if there is no limit to your power, then you will be able to—"

Horns burst from Xavier's head. His teeth lengthened into long, deadly fangs. His skin rippled with scales. Bands of fire wrapped around his fingers and hovered over Mercy. The beast that he was—the beast he kept chained because he knew how horrifying he truly was—that beast clawed and hacked his way to the surface.

Power surged from him and poured into Mercy even as he clamped his mouth around her throat and *bit.* He bit her, and his scaled hand remained pressed to her mouth. His blood would go into her as he bit her. She'd take his power.

He was the king of destruction. He would not lose her, even if he had to fucking destroy the gates of heaven in order to get her back. She would not die. She would not—

Mercy sucked in a deep gulp of air as her body jolted. Immediately, Xavier yanked his mouth from her throat as he looked at her face.

Mercy's eyes flew open. She stared at him.

He started to smile at her.

Then he saw the horror and fear in her gaze.

His hand whipped back from her, and Mercy screamed as she surged upward toward him.

"Mercy? Mercy, it's me! I just look—" Xavier stopped. *Like I really am.*

She collapsed back against the bed. It swung to the left and right.

"Mercy!" Xavier reached out for her.

But Micah grabbed his hands. "She's healing, my king! Look!"

She was. The horrible wound on her wrist—*from my bite and the bastard's knife*—was closing. The ghostly pallor of her skin deepened to a more natural tone. Her breath flowed easily.

"She's healing," Micah said again.

Xavier's head sagged forward. She'd come back. And the first thing she'd done had been to look at him and scream.

She is afraid of me. At her core, she's terrified. She will always be.

"Her shine is gone, but she still lives." Micah let go of Xavier and pressed his fingers to Mercy's neck. "Her pulse is strong. You don't have to worry about her. She'll be okay." He sent Xavier a relieved smile. "Good as new."

Xavier flinched.

"I mean—"

Xavier turned away. His hands clenched into fists, and the deep claws on the ends of his fingers drew blood as he walked toward the broken window. Glass crunched beneath his feet. He stared into the now gray sky and saw...

His dragons. Rushing toward him. Two of them. And they were tossing something back and forth with their mouths. Catching it, releasing it, burning it a bit and...

Whoosh.

The dragons flew toward the castle window.

"Not again!" Micah screamed. "I don't want to ride you! Stay away from me!"

The dragons threw their toy through the window and flew away. They barely even slowed down. Micah watched the toy roll across the room. Shaking. Burning a bit. A big, black cloak covered the toy.

"I'm really fucking sick of unwelcome guests," Xavier rumbled. What the hell was up with that? *His* kingdom. *His* power. So how the hell had—

The cloak vanished. A slightly burned Paxton stared up at him. "I'm here to save you!" After that announcement, Paxton flinched. "Fuck me, the truth hurts."

Yes, it did. Literally.

Paxton bounded to his feet. "There's a changeling coming after you. The tricky sonofabitch has an enchanted iron knife. If we don't stop him, he could hurt you and take your descendant and—" He broke off because he'd just caught sight of the figure on the bed. He stared at Mercy a moment, and sadness pulled at his face. "Is it me, or is your descendant no longer shining?"

Rage pooled in Xavier's gut. *"You* sent the changeling here. You gave him a coin to enter my world." He should obliterate Paxton. Fire began to dance around his fingers.

"I didn't know he was a changeling! Okay, fine, I didn't know when I *first* talked to him. Shit!

Did *you* know? And I sure as hell didn't know that he had a blade that could actually do permanent damage to you, at least not until he killed one of my sweet snakes." A heaving breath. Paxton's gaze remained on Mercy. "Oh, Xavier, what did you do? The way you were so protective with her, I thought you...I thought you might break the curse." He flinched and rubbed his stomach.

"I did break it. She gave up her life for me, but I brought her back." Helpless, his gaze swung to the bed. To Mercy. "She's so afraid of me."

"Uh...you *do* understand all the parts of the curse, yes?" Paxton asked him.

He ignored his brother. "She doesn't shine. She's completely human now."

Paxton cleared his throat. "Does she *look* human?"

She looked like heaven. "Mercy shouldn't be trapped with a monster. She can be free now. No one will hunt her. She doesn't shine. She can go home." He stalked back to the bed. His form shifted so that he looked...

Like a man. The way I want her to see me. Tall. Strong. Handsome.

His fingers slid down her cheek. "I'm a nightmare."

Micah inched to his side. "The worst nightmare, my king. The most wicked."

"Stop being such a yes-man, Micah," Paxton muttered. "No one likes that shit."

Xavier ignored them both. His focus remained on Mercy. "I can be her nightmare. She can wake up, and she can forget me. I can be the nightmare that fades with dawn."

Silence.

Her skin was so smooth.

She died moments before. I know she died. I just didn't let her go. My power—dark, dangerous power—brought her back.

But she deserved better than a life of darkness. "Take her back to her world, Paxton."

"Uh, and I take orders from you because...?"

"Because you fucking gave a changeling a pass to enter my realm. You owe me." He didn't look away from Mercy. He wanted to drink her in. To remember her forever. "Take Mercy back to her world. Give her the best dream you've got. Make that her life."

Paxton clapped.

What?

Xavier spun toward him, and Paxton's eyes were all but gleaming. Like that wasn't weird as fuck. "What the hell is wrong with you?" Xavier demanded.

"You're letting her go...because you think that's best for her."

It was best. She didn't belong in a world of paranormal predators. She could be happy. Have a human family. Enjoy her life. "Give her the best dream, and I'll forget you nearly got me killed."

Paxton slipped around him. He scooped Mercy into his arms.

Xavier tensed. From the corner of his eye, he saw Micah watching him.

"Make sure your dragons don't attack us," Paxton said. "Being a chew toy for them once was bad enough. I don't want to go through that shit twice."

"They won't touch her. She's got my blood in her. They'll smell me. Know she's mine." *No matter where she goes, I'll always think of her as mine.*

Paxton smiled down at Mercy. "She's really quite lovely."

Rage turned his vision red. "You so much as *think* of getting involved with her, and I will rip your dick off and shove it down your throat— while it is on fire."

"Oh, yes." Paxton nodded. "You'll definitely be fine with her living a life without you. No jealousy issues at all."

Xavier growled.

"Do you happen to have a giant mirror handy?" Paxton asked as he continued to hold Mercy. "Unlike you, I don't snap my fingers and teleport. Your fucking wishing wells also still don't work for me so I have to do things old school." A long sigh. "Just direct me toward a powerful, reflective surface, would you? One preferably that has been cursed by a dark witch."

Micah pointed toward the door. "There's a magic mirror in the room next door."

"Of course, there is. Thanks so much." He sauntered away with Mercy in his arms.

Xavier took an automatic step after them, then stopped.

"It didn't hurt?" Micah asked, his voice hushed.

Xavier glared at him. "Of course, it fucking hurt when that prick Thomas drove his knife into my back over and over and severed my spine." The second time in just a few days that he'd had damage to his spine. So freaking annoying.

"No, my king, I mean...giving her up. Letting her go so she could have a normal life. It didn't hurt?"

Xavier lifted his hand and rubbed his chest.

"Because that was something *good*." Micah looked worried. "You hurt when you do something good. Or at least, you used to hurt..."

Xavier's hand pressed harder to his chest. "Trust me, I hurt." But it wasn't the same kind of pain he usually felt with any *good* act. This one was different. This one...this one made him feel as if someone had ripped out his very heart.

Oh, wait. Someone did. I'm that someone. He'd sent Mercy away.

He had given her up. "Get out, Micah." Fire began to swirl.

"But my evil king, she's—"

"Out!"

Micah ran. As soon as the door slammed behind him, fire erupted. It consumed the bed. It raced across the floor. It rushed up the walls. And in the middle of the inferno, Xavier fell to his knees...

I wanted to keep her.

No, no.

I love her.

The flames raged higher.

CHAPTER TWELVE

"A dream is just a nightmare in a sweet and tempting disguise. Don't be fooled."

-Life (and Death) Lessons from Xavier Hollow

"You look beautiful." Her stepfather beamed at her. "An absolute angel in the flesh."

Mercy blinked at her reflection in the mirror. At first, the image before her seemed foggy, oddly distorted, but when she blinked a second time, things came into sharp focus for her.

She wore an angel costume. A silky, long white dress that hugged her body. And big, feathered angel wings were perched on her back.

"Stunning." He sniffed. "You remind me so much of your mother. She'd be incredibly proud of you." He swiped a hand near his eye. "Now, I need to get down to the ball. Don't forget, you agreed to help me out with the auction. But don't worry. You'll be the first charity date, and it will be over in a flash." He turned for the door. "I know how you hate crowds, but it will truly only be for a moment."

The door closed behind him. She kept staring at the mirror. Tonight...tonight was the charity ball. "I wanted to be a witch," Mercy whispered. So why was she dressed as an angel?

A dull ache pounded behind her left eye. She was upstairs, in the dressing room of the old building in New Orleans. In a few moments, she was supposed to go downstairs.

Be friendly. Circulate.

But since when was I supposed to be in the auction? Mercy didn't remember agreeing to that. Things seemed fuzzy in her mind.

She caught sight of the champagne flute nearby. Ah, right. She *had* been nervous about the crowd. Maybe the champagne was the reason things were fuzzy. Lifting up the hem of her dress, Mercy hurried for the door. She almost fell flat on her face, though, when her left ankle decided to twist. Mercy glared at the ridiculously high heels. Why in the world would she have thought those were a good idea?

Now she'd have to be extra careful. Even on a good day, she was clumsy as hell. Her hand grabbed the doorknob, and she wrenched the door open. Mercy headed into the hallway, and then made her way toward the small balcony that overlooked the ballroom. She wanted to get a peek at the guests.

Something kept nagging at her.

Her hands reached out for the balcony's elaborate railing. She leaned forward a bit, and thought...

Where are you?

And she realized that she was searching for someone.

***

"There's something you should know."

Xavier sat on his throne and tossed balls of fire aimlessly into the air.

Micah shuffled forward. "I, ah, found some old volumes in the library. About descendants. They don't *have* to die after their shine is taken. It's just the vicious beasts who enjoy ripping them apart that cause their deaths. Totally unnecessary. They can be drained and then go on to enjoy normal human lives."

Xavier tossed more fire.

"It was something Paxton said that made me really curious and got me to keep digging. He acted as if you didn't know the full curse your father had placed upon you."

"Paxton is a liar."

"Yes, he is, your most wicked. Absolutely, you're correct on that score." Micah nervously wet his lips. "But I noticed your brother flinched. Like he was in pain. He *flinched*, and I think he was telling the truth about the curse." A long exhale. "So I kept looking and found a little more."

There was no "more" to find. Xavier knew all about the curse. How could he not? His father had taunted him with it many times. "My twisted devil of a father wanted to drain all the good from me. So he wanted me to destroy someone good." *I almost did*. No, he had. She'd been dead. The world had been dark. Everything had been dark and—

"You had three days to do it."

The balls swirled. "Goal accomplished." Where was Mercy? Had she already forgotten him? Was she happy? Maybe he should just snap over to the human world to make sure she was safe. What would a quick snap hurt?

Stop it. You hurt. You destroy. That's all you do. Stay away from her.

"Three days to destroy someone good...or have someone good sacrifice herself for you. We thought that was the same thing."

"I'm bored." Xavier threw a ball at Micah's feet.

Micah easily dodged the flames. "She sacrificed for you, but *you* sacrificed for her, too. You gave her your power, then you let her go. You sent her away so that she'd be safe. So that she'd have a normal life."

With someone else. Someone who will get to touch her and love her and—

He tossed a ball of flames straight upward. The flames left a gaping hole in the glass ceiling. He ignored the chunks of glass that rained down on him.

Micah dodged the falling glass. "Your father wanted you to be a creature that only destroys. But even as you broke the curse, you became something else."

Xavier rose to his feet. "Enough of this. Do you want me to burn every—"

"You kept me. You protected me. You became my family." Micah lifted his chin. "You love me like I'm an annoying little brother. But you love her like she's your whole world."

Xavier did not speak.

"If you just destroy, you can't love. But you *do* love. You love so much that you sacrifice for others. *You* broke the curse. Not her. You did it because you said fuck you to his rules and you took the pain that came from doing a good deed. You *died* for her, didn't you? And don't even think about lying. The panthers were watching, and they told me. She poured her blood and shine down your dead throat and brought you back."

He didn't exactly know what the hell had happened. One moment, he'd been in total darkness. Drifting. Lost. And then...*an explosion of light*. "So what?"

Micah's eyes widened. "You don't...you don't feel pain when you do good deeds any longer, do you? When you let her go, it hurt, but it hurt because your heart was breaking, not because you did something good."

"So. What?"

Micah grabbed him. "So why is she in the human world and you are here? Why are you denying yourself what you want most? You still have all your power. You can have her, too. Why would you be away from her? *Why?*"

"Because she is afraid of me." A humiliating truth. "And I cannot stand to see the fear in her eyes." He transformed before Micah. The full scales. The horns. The fucking tail. The talons that were made to rip and eviscerate. "This is who I am. She should have more."

More than a scale-covered body.

Twisted and taloned-tipped wings.

A beast with a mouthful of fangs.

"That isn't who you are." Micah glared up at him. "Turn back. *Now.*"

Surprised by the sharp order, Xavier did.

"*This* is you. This form. The other one is just the armor you wear when your enemies are close."

Micah was so wrong. "There was no enemy when I transformed before her in that bedroom—"

But Micah nodded. "Yes, there was. Death was there. And you were ready to rip him apart if it meant you could keep Mercy breathing. I pushed you to transform then because I suspected what you were facing. But that was just your battle gear. *This* is who you are."

"No."

"Yes! The monster is a disguise you wear. Paxton is the one who lives to lie. Not you. So don't you think it's time to stop pretending? Stop lying to yourself?"

His gaze fell. "She was scared of me. Terrified. Horror filled her eyes."

"Are you sure? Are you *sure* she feared you? Because a woman doesn't die for a man she fears."

"I'm not a man."

"My wicked, wicked king...that's utter bullshit."

***

He's not here.

She felt it, knew it, and had no idea who *he* even was. Mercy turned away from the balcony, and she hurried toward the stairs. She'd go down to the first level and join the costumed ball. But she'd only taken a few steps when she lost her footing—those damn heels—and began to tumble.

"Got you." A man caught her before she could fall and break her bones. Tall. Dressed in a black suit. With a black mask over the upper part of his face.

Relief swept through her. "Thank you!" A wide smile curved her lips, but her smile froze when she looked into his blue eyes.

"Is something wrong?" he asked.

Yes. "Wrong color."

His grip tightened on her. "Excuse me?"

"Your eyes should be dark." She pulled away from him. "Thank you for helping me." She tried to slide around him, but her wings were so big and bulky that they took up all the room on the stairs. She wound up hitting him with a wing before she eased down a step.

"Can't have an angel falling. That would be a nightmare."

She stilled. His voice seemed familiar to her. Mercy glanced back. "Do I know you?" Perhaps he was one of her stepfather's friends.

"You've never met me," he told her cheerfully.

"Oh. Sorry." She carefully climbed down a few more steps. She could feel his gaze on her, but Mercy didn't look back. She needed to get down to the ball. A force drove her to search the crowd. To look for someone. *A man with dark eyes.*

And that was silly.

She stood in the middle of the ballroom as couples swirled and danced around her and had the thought that...*We never had our dance.*

Mercy shook her head.

"Mercy!" Her stepfather appeared. He caught her hand. "You're supposed to be on stage. The bidding is starting!"

Bidding. The charity dates. Right. All vaguely familiar. Moments later, she found herself led onto the stage. A spotlight shone on her. And she gazed into the crowd of masked attendees.

Where is he?

Her hand slid over her dress, smoothing down the fabric, and she realized that there was a small pocket on the right side of her dress. So tiny. Barely detectable. Her fingers dipped into the pocket.

She pulled out a gleaming, silver coin.

The light hit the coin.

A woman's cheerful voice called out, "Welcome to our charity auction! Shall we get ready to—"

Mercy kicked off her shoes and leapt off the stage.

Her father rushed toward her. "Mercy!"

"I love you." She hugged him. Tight. "But there is somewhere else I have to be." The image of an old wishing well was in her mind—*his well*—and she raced away from her stepfather as gasps followed in her wake.

***

"What is it that you want?" Micah demanded. "For her to somehow *choose* you? To come back to you? Is that why you're sitting here and moping?"

"I am not moping." The suggestion was fucking insulting. And...true.

"She can't come back! She doesn't have a coin! Your brother probably took away her memory and gave her some beautiful dream life that doesn't involve you. If you want her, *go get her.*"

He wanted her more than he wanted anything else in this world or any other. That was why he had let her go. *I love her too much to force her to stay with me.*

"My devious and dastardly king, I can't help but notice you are not moving."

"If she comes back to me, I'd make her immortal."

Micah nodded. "Of course. You'd bring in the most powerful witches. You'd get her to be bonded with you forever. The whole glorious mating ceremony that we haven't seen in centuries for a king of your caliber."

"She'd never be free of me. I wouldn't be able to let her go again." He knew it, with utter certainty. "Humans don't realize how long forever truly is." His gaze took in the dark and gloomy throne room. "Would you want to spend forever here?"

"There is no place I'd rather be."

"You were born a werewolf. Not a human. And she's not made for this place—"

"But my most cruel and twisted king—"

"I want her happy!" A roar. "She chooses her path. Not me. I will not take her life away from her." Then, softer, "Not again. I can't do that to her again..."

CHAPTER THIRTEEN

"Do monsters love? Nah. Forget that. Better question. Who can love a monster?"

-Life (and Death) Lessons from Xavier Hollow

The restaurant was closed and empty. Probably because it was nearing midnight. Mercy grabbed the wrought-iron gates that led to the courtyard, and she shoved them with all of her might. More of the stupid feathers from her wings fluttered in the air. Those wings had been battered to hell and back during her frantic journey across town and to the restaurant.

I have to get to him.

Another shove, and the gates crashed open. There were two pairs of gates at the restaurant that waited in the heart of New Orleans. One near the front entrance that took you into the building. And another pair of gates that led straight to the courtyard. The back gates.

She rushed through the back gates. It was so dark in that courtyard. The vines overhead stretched and stretched and blocked out the starlight. But she went unerringly to the well. Her left hand slapped against the stones as her right opened to reveal the silver coin she still carried. Her eyes closed. "I wish—"

Something clamped around her right wrist. "Not so fast."

A gasp tore from her. Her eyes flew open even as her head whipped toward the voice.

Lights flashed on above her. A hundred gleaming, hanging bulbs.

"Haven't you heard...?" The stranger from the ball stood beside her. The mask still partially covered his face as he held her wrist. "It's dangerous to trust the devil."

She yanked her hand away from him. "You followed me."

He smiled at her. "When you raced from the ball as if the hounds of hell were on your heels, I suspected you would be coming here. No need to follow you. I just *met* you here."

Her breath came faster. Her heart seemed in jeopardy of racing out of her chest. "We've...been here before."

"You shouldn't remember that."

"You..." Hazy images. Everything seemed to be foggy inside her mind. "You stopped me before."

"Um, I tried to help you make the right choice back then, but you ignored me." A sigh. "And here I am again, being amazing, and trying to tell you that the devil is not the one you want."

The devil. A chill skated down her spine. "This is the Devil's Wishing Well."

"According to some." His head tilted. His blue eyes turned curious. "Why did you run here?" But then his gaze fell to her hand. In a flash, he'd grabbed it again. He gently pried open her fingers to reveal the coin. "Ah." A nod. "Didn't realize you had that on you. Probably really screwed up my illusion."

The chill grew worse. "Excuse me?"

"He wanted you to have a perfect life. The best dream." The stranger winced. "Truth fucking hurts."

She did not follow what he was saying. At all.

"Having the coin meant you were still linked to him. He's still drifting around in your mind, isn't he? That's why you ran here. You probably remember bits and pieces, just not the whole thing."

She did. Bits and pieces. "I think I flew on a dragon."

He laughed. "Doubtful. No beast would ever let someone like you fly. Absolutely crazy. You say stuff like that, and you might as well say that you see monsters." A faint grimace ended those words.

I do. Her stomach twisted. "I do see them. I'm not crazy." She wasn't crazy. She was *not*. Mercy pushed against the shadows in her mind. Once more, her fingers closed around the coin. "He told me I wasn't crazy. It was all true."

"He, huh? Who is this magical person? Don't know his name, do you?"

No, she didn't. "Shadows." That was what she saw in her mind. And when she saw monsters, she saw shadows, too.

"Give me the coin, and I'll make a trade with you. You can keep your illusion. You can have

what you really want. And what you want? It's a
normal life. One where you marry a boring
human. Have lots of kids running about. It's one
where you never think about monsters again.
Sound good?"

She opened her hand and looked down at the
coin.

"I fixed everything from before. No one
remembers the werewolf attack at the ball. Hell, I
did an entire redo of the scene. Like it never
happened. That's why you were there tonight. You
don't have to ever meet him. He can never be in
your life. You'll be better off without him. He'll be
better off without you."

He.

Still no name. She wanted a name. She
wanted—

A gasp slid from her. "The truth fucking
hurts."

"Um."

"You—*you meant that. I-I remember. The
truth hurts you.*"

He didn't speak.

So she did. She went back through their whole
conversation. Because while some memories were
clouded in shadows, Mercy remembered the last
five minutes perfectly. "Don't trust the devil.
That's what you said."

His lips thinned. "I actually think I told you it
was *dangerous* to trust the evil."

"But you really meant that I should trust
him." The man in her mind. The man covered in
shadows.

Silence.

"You're giving me a mix of truth and lies. Blending them all together." She had to figure out what was real and what wasn't. "He'll be better off without me."

"Right. Exactly. I told you—"

"That's a lie."

A faint smile curved the stranger's lips. "Is it?"

"You said I'd be better off without him."

"Yes. You can have the normal life you want. It's waiting. It's—"

"An illusion." She turned back toward the well. "I don't want an illusion. I don't want lies. I want my memory back. I want *him* back."

"He's a monster. A beast. He can't love. He will bring you nothing but heartache and pain."

A relieved smile curled her lips. "I'm starting to understand you. There wasn't even a hint of pain in those words. Sometimes, when you talk, it's like you're having to force the words out. That's when you say the truth, right? But the lies roll so easily off your tongue." She stared at the gleaming coin. "He can love. And he is going to bring me joy."

"He can't—"

"I wish to be with the man I love." Because his face might be in shadows, but her heart told her the truth.

The coin fell into the well.

Nothing happened.

Mercy had rather expected something to happen.

The man sighed in disgust. "Seriously? You don't know what happens next?" He shuffled closer. "Do I have to do everything?"

She started to turn toward him.

But he shoved into her and sent her tumbling into the well. A startled scream tore from her.

"You're welcome!" he yelled after her.

***

The sound of a scream had Xavier's head whipping up. He stared at the glass ceiling above him, and he squinted because he could see something hurtling down toward him though the gaping hole his fire had created earlier. "Can just *anyone* get in my kingdom these days?" Rage burned inside of him. If this was another enemy—and it had to be an enemy—he would enjoy this battle. Ripping his enemies apart would be a perfect distraction.

"I...wait...does that look like..." Micah bumped into him. "Is that an angel?"

Crash.

The glass ceiling above him shattered even more as what looked like an angel hurtled into the throne room. Xavier moved instinctively, and he lunged underneath her and opened his arms.

She slammed into his hold and feathers danced in the air around her.

Mercy.

His knees hit the floor.

Her head turned. She stared at him. At first, Mercy looked at him with zero recognition on her face and in her eyes, and his heart lodged into his chest and then—

She smiled. A wide smile that lit her amber eyes and had joy sliding over her face. "There you are!" She locked an arm around his neck and brought him in for a passionate kiss. A deep and consuming and joyous kiss. "I knew you were missing!"

He tumbled back on the floor and didn't care that glass crunched beneath him. Mercy was on top of him, kissing him frantically on the mouth and then moving to rain kisses over his cheeks. She held him in a fierce embrace as her feathers shook loose and fluttered around them.

"I'll just...give you some privacy." Micah's steps beat a hasty retreat.

Xavier locked his hands around Mercy and, for a time, he just pulled her even closer. He took her mouth again. Kissed her with all the longing and need and desperate desire that burned within him. And then— "No!" A thunderous cry.

In a flash, he was off the floor. He'd put her on his throne because he damn well didn't want any glass cutting her. He locked a hand around each arm of the chair and leaned in toward her as he trapped her in that spot. "You should not be here."

Mercy blinked. "Aren't you happy to see me?"

Deliriously so. But now I can't let you go, and you're going to hate me. He studied her carefully as he looked for the fear in her eyes. But there was none.

There was just...love.

"Why was I in New Orleans?" Mercy shook her head. "I was back at the ball. And everything was just rolling along as if my time with you never happened. But it did happen. You happened. You were real. But in my head, there were all of these shadows. I couldn't push past them to see you. Then I found the coin."

She'd found a coin?

"I remembered the well. I went back there. I wished to be with the man I love, and now I'm here." Her hand rose to press to his cheek. "Xavier." Satisfaction rolled in the name. "I remember you."

He had to swallow twice before he could speak. "You were supposed to be safe."

"I'm safe with you."

"You were supposed to be happy."

"I'm happy with you, though I am also really, really pissed because I think you had something to do with me being sent away."

His hands tightened around the arms of his throne. "You don't belong in a world of monsters. *I took your shine. You died. Then you woke up and saw me and you were afraid—*"

"I remember." Her expression turned serious. But still, not afraid. "You didn't take anything. I gave it to you. I wanted you to heal. I needed you to be safe. And, yes, I think I did die."

His whole body shuddered.

"And it was beautiful and peaceful and nothing hurt at all—"

Her words were tearing him apart.

"Until I realized you weren't there. Then it wasn't beautiful because I wanted you, and when I came back and I screamed, it was because I was terrified *you* weren't going to be with me. I screamed because I didn't want to be away from you. I was afraid of losing you. Afraid that I'd stay in the world without you, and I desperately wanted to be with *you*."

Shock stole his breath.

"And when I found myself back in New Orleans, back at the ball...everything was beautiful there, too, and nothing hurt..."

The lump in his throat threatened to choke him.

"Until I realized you weren't there. I didn't have your name, but you were burned in my soul. I missed you and..." Anger flashed in her eyes. "Don't you *ever* do something like that again, do you understand? Sending me away was total bullshit. You don't get to do that ever again. My life. My decisions."

"I'm a *monster*." In a blink, he transformed before her. Into the form that had sent terror flaring in her eyes before. "You deserve a normal man. You deserve a normal life. I was giving you the goodness that you should have—"

She kissed him. Carefully, because he did have a mouthful of fangs. A closed-mouth kiss. A tender kiss.

But she kissed him, and he had no choice but to transform back because...

This is who I am with her. Not a monster. A man.

"You don't scare me," Mercy whispered against his lips. "But a world without you? That terrifies me."

He let go of the throne and grabbed desperately for her. "I can't be good twice. I can't let you go again. I just don't have it in me."

"Excellent. Then be bad. Keep me forever because that's what I intend to do with you. I'm keeping you, Xavier."

He had to make sure she understood. "It will be forever. You'll become immortal with me. I-I can arrange visits back to the human world so you can see your stepfather, but eventually, he will die. You won't. You'll stay with me. Once we are bonded, that's how it becomes for my kind. I'll find the most powerful witch in the world, and she'll link our life forces. We will live and die together." Words that should utterly petrify her.

"You died for me already. And I died for you, too." A little shrug of her shoulders. "I would die for you again."

"Never."

"I don't shine anymore, do I?" A bit of sadness. "Do you not...do you not want me as much without the—"

"You shine so brightly I can't see anything else." The absolute truth. And it wasn't about magic or being a descendant. To him, she glowed because she was...Mercy. His Mercy. "You are the most beautiful thing in my world. In every world."

"You love me?"

"I died for you."

"You did."

But he'd done more than die. "I gave you up." He'd given up the only woman he'd ever loved. *It was like cutting out my own heart one slow slice at a time.*

Mercy shook her head. "A completely unnecessary and annoying sacrifice that made me have to jump into a well again for you. Though, technically, I believe your brother might have *pushed* me into the well at the end."

He tucked a lock of hair behind her ear. "I am the most selfish bastard you will ever meet. I abhor good deeds. I take what I want, and I laugh while the world burns."

She shook her head. "No."

His forehead rested against hers. "I let you go because I wanted you to have the best life possible. I wanted to be more than a selfish bastard when it came to you."

"You are more."

She was his everything.

He knelt in front of her. "Will you be my queen?" Xavier extended his hand toward her and waited.

"Will I be the queen of destruction?"

Xavier shook his head. "No, sweetheart, you don't have that in you."

"Then what will I be?"

"Mercy. Exactly what you've always been. The goodness in the dark. A fitting match for destruction, don't you think?"

Her smile bloomed. "I love you."

He kept his hand extended. "Is that a yes?"

She flew into his arms. *"Yes."*

And he laughed and held her tight because he was truly happy. Happy and loved and he didn't care about any curse.

Fuck the curse.

He had Mercy.

He'd tried to be good, for her. Tried to make a sacrifice, for her. But she'd come back to him.

Now, he would never, ever let her go.

His mouth took hers. His hands slid over her back, but he hit the damn wings. Growling, he jerked them off her back.

Her soft laughter teased his lips. "You've done this before."

He eased away from her, but just for a moment. "Even without wings, you're an angel to me." No pain came with those words. Once upon a time, a compliment would have sent hives chasing over his skin.

He wasn't just giving her a compliment, though. He was giving Mercy the truth. She was his salvation.

His gaze slid down her body. The white dress clung to her shapely form. Had him nearly going crazy because he had missed her so fucking much. Hours had passed, but to him, it had seemed he'd lived a lifetime without her.

He never wanted to go through that hell again.

"When you ditched the wings before, you also helped to get me out of my dress. Partially, anyway."

His stare whipped back up to hers.

"Maybe you could help again? The dress feels so..." Her hand trailed down his chest. "Confining. I also distinctly remember you doing a little trick where you can make clothing vanish."

He did that little trick for her. Her gown vanished. Her panties and bra disappeared. His clothes melted into nothingness. And his control? It vanished, too. He dragged her against him, lifted her up, and plundered her tempting mouth with his own. She kissed him back with a wild fury that he just adored, as he adored everything else about her.

Her legs wrapped around his waist. Her tempting sex pressed against his dick, and all he wanted was to drive right inside of her.

Not yet. Always give Mercy pleasure. Always. No pain for her. His number one rule. The rule that would not ever be broken, or he'd fucking kill someone.

He put her back on the throne.

"No, Xavier—" She reached for him once more.

He knelt in front of her and pushed her thighs apart. Good thing the throne was wide. It let him have plenty of access. His fingers moved to curl around her waist, and he dragged her toward the edge of the throne.

Then he feasted.

She arched and twisted, and her nails dug into his back. He licked and sucked, and his thumb strummed her clit feverishly. Her first orgasm came quickly. She cried out his name as she pushed her core against his mouth.

He didn't stop. He loved tasting her pleasure. And he licked even more. Drove his tongue into her and felt her tremble over and over again.

"Xavier, stop the torture!"

His head lifted. "Not torture, sweetheart. Never with you. Only pleasure."

Her breath panted out. "Make love to me."

He was. Always would.

He picked her up, spun her around, and he sat on the throne, with her in his lap. She straddled his thighs, and she grabbed the arms of the chair to balance herself. Then his Mercy slowly lowered onto his eager dick.

The only heaven I know is with her. Without her, he would have been condemned to hell.

He lodged in her fully, but, for a moment, he didn't move at all. He just stared into Mercy's amber eyes.

"Have I ever told you..." She licked her lips. "How sexy it is when your eyes go red?"

He blinked.

She dipped her head forward, and this time, she licked *his* lips. "So sexy."

She didn't mind his red eyes. She laughed when he turned into a dragon and flew through the sky. She kissed him when he was a beast.

She owned him. Body. Heart. All that he was. Every dark sliver.

His hands lifted her hips. Brought her down. Lifted. The pace was wild and remorseless. Primitive and consuming. When she came again, Mercy tossed back her head and screamed her release.

He was afraid he held her too tightly, so he grabbed for the throne chair arms even as she slumped against him. He drove into her again and again. Pleasure built. The climax grew closer. His Mercy.

"Bite me," she whispered.

He did.

Pleasure. A world of pleasure. Paradise. So much joy.

Mercy.

He exploded within her as the orgasm took him. She cried out again. Only pleasure. Her delicate inner muscles contracted greedily around his cock.

They both flew into oblivion.

And, then, a few moments later, they both crashed onto the floor...because they'd broken the throne.

Mercy laughed and levered herself up as she looked down at him. He still lodged within her, and he didn't give a damn about the shattered throne beneath him.

"You good?" she asked him.

His hands slid to her waist. "Parts of me."

A furrow appeared between her brows.

"Because of you, parts of me are good." He pulled her down to him so he could kiss her mouth. "But parts of me will always be very, very wicked." Fair warning.

"That's okay. I like you wicked." She nipped his lower lip. "I can be wicked, too."

Oh, he'd love to see that.

Luckily, he had an eternity to spend with her. There would be plenty of time to see Mercy's wicked side come out to play.

"Sorry about your throne," she whispered.

"Fuck it. I'll get another. Two of them. One for you. One for me." Because he would rule with her. This was their kingdom.

Their world.

Destruction and Mercy.

And he started to fuck her again.

No, he started to make love to her again...

And again...

And again...

EPILOGUE

"They lived wickedly and evilly ever after. And if anyone so much as glared at his queen...the king of destruction cut his eyes out.
What? Too gory? Who cares? I'm leaving that in the damn guide."

-Life (and Death) Lessons from Xavier Hollow

Micah glanced up at the dark sky. "Two minutes until midnight." He hummed. And *that* was how you broke a curse.

He smiled.

A dragon circled overhead.

Micah tensed. "Don't even think of coming down here to blow fire my way or to take a bite..."

But the dragon circled lower.

Shit, shit, shit...

The dragon landed. And he lowered his head before Micah. "I'll be damned!" Was the dragon offering him a ride?

The dragon didn't move. Micah inched closer. "You breathe fire at me, and you'll be sorry. The king is my best friend..."

The dragon snorted, but didn't blow fire. Not this time. This time, he just waited.

Micah scrambled onto his back. The dragon launched into the sky. *I'm riding an untamed dragon!* Laughter burst from his lips.

Micah had the feeling that things were going to be different in this world now that the curse was broken and Mercy was home.

Home. This was her home, he knew it. And he thought she did, too. She'd come back for Xavier, she'd fought for him, and in the end...

It hadn't been her shine that had been important.

It had just been her.

The dragon flew higher.

And Micah laughed louder.

THE END

A NOTE FROM THE AUTHOR

I love paranormal romances. Love writing about characters who have wild powers and magical strength. Paranormal stories push the limits. Anything can happen in these books—and anything usually does happen.

Give me a monster. Give me the villain. And then let's see about redeeming that bad guy. Because it's the bad guys that are so much fun.

I hope you enjoyed MONSTER WITHOUT MERCY.

If you'd like to stay updated on my releases and sales, please join my newsletter list.

https://cynthiaeden.com/newsletter/

Thank you for reading MONSTER WITHOUT MERCY.

Best,
Cynthia Eden
cynthiaeden.com

ABOUT THE AUTHOR

Cynthia Eden is a *New York Times, USA Today, Digital Book World,* and *IndieReader* bestselling author of romantic suspense and paranormal romance. She's a prolific author who lives along the Alabama Gulf Coast. In her free time, you'll find her reading romances, watching horror movies, or hunting for adventures. She's a chocolate addict and a major *Supernatural* fan.

For More Information
- *cynthiaeden.com*
- *facebook.com/cynthiaedenfanpage*

HER OTHER WORKS

Ice Breaker Cold Case Romance
- Frozen In Ice (Book 1)
- Falling For The Ice Queen (Book 2)
- Ice Cold Saint (Book 3)
- Touched By Ice (Book 4)
- Trapped In Ice (Book 5)
- Forged From Ice (Book 6)
- Buried Under Ice (Book 7)

Wilde Ways
- Protecting Piper (Book 1)
- Guarding Gwen (Book 2)
- Before Ben (Book 3)
- The Heart You Break (Book 4)
- Fighting For Her (Book 5)
- Ghost Of A Chance (Book 6)
- Crossing The Line (Book 7)
- Counting On Cole (Book 8)
- Chase After Me (Book 9)
- Say I Do (Book 10)
- Roman Will Fall (Book 11)
- The One Who Got Away (Book 12)
- Pretend You Want Me (Book 13)
- Cross My Heart (Book 14)
- The Bodyguard Next Door (Book 15)

- Ex Marks The Perfect Spot (Book 16)
- The Thief Who Loved Me (Book 17)

Wilde Ways: Gone Rogue

- How To Protect A Princess (Book 1)
- How To Heal A Heartbreak (Book 2)
- How To Con A Crime Boss (Book 3)

Trouble For Hire

- No Escape From War (Book 1)
- Don't Play With Odin (Book 2)
- Jinx, You're It (Book 3)
- Remember Ramsey (Book 4)

Death and Moonlight Mystery

- Step Into My Web (Book 1)
- Save Me From The Dark (Book 2)

Phoenix Fury

- Hot Enough To Burn (Book 1)
- Slow Burn (Book 2)
- Burn It Down (Book 3)

Dark Sins

- Don't Trust A Killer (Book 1)
- Don't Love A Liar (Book 2)

Lazarus Rising

- Never Let Go (Book One)
- Keep Me Close (Book Two)
- Stay With Me (Book Three)
- Run To Me (Book Four)
- Lie Close To Me (Book Five)
- Hold On Tight (Book Six)

Bad Things

- The Devil In Disguise (Book 1)
- On The Prowl (Book 2)
- Undead Or Alive (Book 3)
- Broken Angel (Book 4)
- Heart Of Stone (Book 5)
- Tempted By Fate (Book 6)
- Wicked And Wild (Book 7)
- Saint Or Sinner (Book 8)

Bite Series

- Forbidden Bite (Bite Book 1)
- Mating Bite (Bite Book 2)

Blood and Moonlight Series

- Bite The Dust (Book 1)
- Better Off Undead (Book 2)
- Bitter Blood (Book 3)

Mine Series

- Mine To Take (Book 1)
- Mine To Keep (Book 2)
- Mine To Hold (Book 3)
- Mine To Crave (Book 4)
- Mine To Have (Book 5)
- Mine To Protect (Book 6)

Dark Obsession Series

- Watch Me (Book 1)
- Want Me (Book 2)
- Need Me (Book 3)
- Beware Of Me (Book 4)
- Only For Me (Books 1 to 4)

Purgatory Series

- The Wolf Within (Book 1)
- Marked By The Vampire (Book 2)
- Charming The Beast (Book 3)
- Deal with the Devil (Book 4)
- The Beasts Inside (Books 1 to 4)

Bound Series

- Bound By Blood (Book 1)
- Bound In Darkness (Book 2)
- Bound In Sin (Book 3)
- Bound By The Night (Book 4)
- Bound in Death (Book 5)
- Forever Bound (Books 1 to 4)

Stand-Alone Romantic Suspense

- Waiting For Christmas
- Kiss Me This Christmas
- It's A Wonderful Werewolf
- Never Cry Werewolf
- Immortal Danger
- Deck The Halls
- Come Back To Me
- Put A Spell On Me
- Never Gonna Happen
- One Hot Holiday
- Slay All Day
- Midnight Bite
- Secret Admirer
- Christmas With A Spy
- Femme Fatale
- Until Death
- Sinful Secrets
- First Taste of Darkness

- **A Vampire's Christmas Carol**

Made in the USA
Las Vegas, NV
04 November 2023

80252291R00115